HOW I  NICKY FLYNN FINALLY GET A LIFE (AND A DOG)

HOW I NICKY FLYNN FINALLY GET A LIFE (AND A DOG)

A NOVEL BY
ART CORRIVEAU

AMULET BOOKS · NEW YORK

The Library of Congress has cataloged the hardcover edition of this book as follows:

Corriveau, Art.
How I, Nicky Flynn, finally get a life (and a dog) / by Art Corriveau.
p. cm.
Summary: Moving to inner-city Boston after his parents' divorce, eleven-year-old Nicky struggles to cope with the changes in his life, including acquiring a former guide dog that leads to a mystery for Nicky to solve.
ISBN 978-0-8109-8298-7
[1. German shepherd dog—Fiction. 2. Dogs—Fiction. 3. Guide dogs—Fiction. 4. Divorce—Fiction. 5. Moving, Household—Fiction. 6. Boston (Mass.)—Fiction. 7. Mystery and detective stories.] I. Title.
PZ7.C81658Se 2010
[Fic]—dc22
2009022935

ISBN 978-0-8109-9687-8

ABRAMS
THE ART OF BOOKS SINCE 1949
115 West 18th Street
New York, NY 10011
www.abramsbooks.com

FOR TIM
(AND CHIMA)

PART ONE

YOU CAN'T TEACH
AN OLD DOG NEW TRICKS

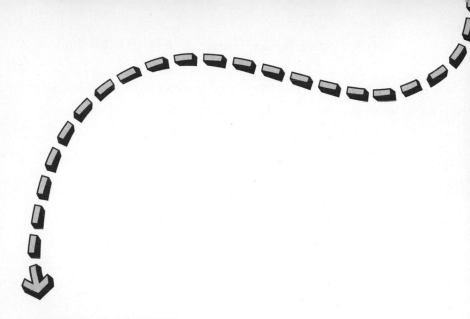

FRIDAY NIGHT. THE NEW APARTMENT.

We have this dog now.

His name is Reggie.

Don't look at me, I didn't name him. My mom got him at the pound yesterday. That's the way pound dogs come: already named. Supposedly, it's too late to change this one's name from Reggie to something more doglike, like, say, Trooper or Flash or Blitzkrieg, because it would confuse him. Or, at least, that's what Mom says the pound told *her*.

Then again, she lies.

"Take him back," I told her.

Mom was *supposed* to be bringing stuff home from the Supa-Sava to make tacos with. But she wasn't holding a bag of groceries—just a leash, with Reggie hooked to the other end. "This apartment is way too small for a dog," I told her. And it's totally true. I'm sleeping on a foldout sofa in the living room. There's barely enough room for the two of us without adding a big, drooly pound dog into the mix, especially one that looks all sad and sort of embarrassed about his name.

"Guess what, Nicky?" Mom said.

(That's me, Nicky Flynn, though technically speaking, my name is Nicholas. But nobody ever calls me that except her—and only when she's mad.)

"I hate guessing," I said.

"Reggie used to be a seeing-eye dog," she said. "Isn't that great?"

"So why isn't he working for some blind guy?" I said.

Seeing-eye dog my foot. I'm nobody's fool. In fact, you wouldn't believe what I've been through. Mom says I'm way too serious for a kid my age. She says I'm like this forty-year-old man trapped in an eleven-year-old body. Yeah, well, believe me, if I were a real forty-year-old, there'd be a few changes around here. P.S., I'm eleven and three-quarters.

"I guess it didn't work out," Mom said.

"What did he do?" I said.

She didn't have the details. The pound doesn't give those out. All they would tell her was that Reggie was a full-blooded German shepherd, which is supposedly one of the smartest breeds out there. I gave him the once-over. He didn't look all that smart to me. Just sad. He did look like a German shepherd, though; I'll give him that much.

"Take him back," I said.

"But you've always wanted a dog," she said.

"I've always wanted a pool table. But the landlord's not going to allow *that* up here either," I said. Our landlord lives right below us. He's always telling me to pick up my feet and turn down the TV. I never even thought about my feet where we used to live. We had a big house of our own and we could say or do whatever we wanted.

"I already asked," Mom said. "The landlord told me a dog was OK, as long as it wasn't too big and didn't make a mess of the new carpet."

We both looked over at Reggie. He must go eighty pounds, easy.

"Let's just give it a few days," Mom said.

And that was that. She led Reggie into the living room— *my* room—and told him to make himself at home. He sniffed around a little, then whined. "What's the matter, boy?" Mom said. "Are you hungry?"

That's when she remembered about the groceries.

We ended up going to Taco Mucho over in the strip mall. We drove-thru and ate in the parking lot, with the public radio station on so we could catch the rest of the news. Reggie just sat there in the backseat, panting. Maybe he guessed we would stop off at the Supa-Sava on the way home to buy him a can of dog food. Or maybe he just knew better than to beg any tacos off of *me*.

◼◼◼

A LITTLE BACKGROUND INFO . . .

L ike I said, my mom lies.

Which is why I decided to start this mental log of when and where and how. That's what Dr. Ice, my secret favorite cartoon crime-fighter, does whenever he's keeping tabs on his archenemies, the Heat. Technically speaking, I'm a little old for Dr. Ice. But I'm sick and tired of Mom getting off scot-free with everything she says.

Here's a list of a whole bunch of stuff she told me this past summer that just isn't true. She said, for instance, that we'd be much better off living here in Boston than out in the suburbs. I can already tell you after just three weeks here: We're not.

First of all, Charlestown isn't Boston. You can sort of *see* Boston from Charlestown, if you squint through a bunch of highway overpasses and bridges. But Charlestown itself is pretty much exactly what it says—a town named Charles— not much bigger than Littleton, where I'm from. About the only difference is that Charlestown's a lot more run-down and dirty. Plus the buildings are all squished together in rows, which they call town houses, even though the houses where *I'm* from in a real town have big front and back lawns with lots of trees. We now live in a one-bedroom apartment on the parlor level (which is the first-and-a-half floor) of one of these so-called town houses on Eden Street. Eden is supposedly the beautiful garden where Adam and Eve lived when they named all the animals. About all they could name here in Charlestown are alley cats and squirrels. And Adam would have to sleep in the middle of the living room, just like me.

Back in Littleton we used to own a *real* house on King Street, a big, white one with green shutters. I had my own room with a door that locked.

Plus I went to fifth grade at this really great elementary school in Littleton Common that had a campus with a swimming pool, an auditorium, and a computer lab. In fact, I was just about to ask my best friend, Marky, if he wanted to try out for junior high soccer when—ZAP!— Mom tells me out of the blue in mid-August that she's put the house on the market and rented an apartment in the city. I had the worst Labor Day weekend ever. While Marky was barbecuing hot dogs and hamburgers in his backyard, I was actually, you know, *laboring*. I can't tell you how many boxes of old clothes and toys I schlepped out of my room, into the car, and over to Goodwill. The very next Tuesday, I found myself walking through the doors of this totally sketchy middle school in Charlestown you'd swear was a maximum-security prison if you didn't read the sign. Forget about sixth-grade soccer. My new school doesn't even have *grass*. It only took about a week for everybody in class to realize I'm, like, a half a grade ahead when it comes to math and reading. *Me.* So now everybody thinks I'm some kind of book freak and nobody will talk to me.

In Littleton I was just a normal kid who had tons of friends. Well, maybe not tons. But lots.

But that's not what this log is about. It's about Mom's lying.

Here's another example: Mom swears this new apartment is a lot less work than that big old house. Oh yeah? So how come there's always dishes in the sink and dust kitties under the table? Big fat one. She loved our old house. Plus she had this gigantic flower garden she was really proud of. She spent half the day out there, digging and humming and pruning her roses. She doesn't ever hum here in the city, and the one potted plant she brought with her—the philodendron from our front hallway—isn't looking so hot.

Example number three: Mom likes her new job. She's always telling her old friends back home how much she loves standing on her own two feet. As if! She just sits at a desk all day, answering the phone for these two lawyers downtown—that father-and-son team you constantly see on TV, shouting at you to give their 800 number a call if you've been hurt on the job or involved in a bad car accident. Mom calls them the Ambulance Chasers behind their backs. She's told all her Littleton friends she likes hearing *other* people's hard-luck stories for a change. Whenever they call to see how she's doing, she tells them all about the mailman who slipped on an icy sidewalk, the old lady who got run over at a crosswalk, or some hospital patient who had the wrong parts taken out. Mom's favorite stories seem to be about wives who take their husbands to the cleaners for cheating on them. Back in my old neighborhood, whenever anyone cheated at kickball, we just stopped playing with them.

Anyway, if work is such a barrel of laughs all day long, why is Mom so tired when she gets home? All she ever wants to do is flop in front of the TV in the living room with a glass of white wine and watch nature shows until I finally wake her up so *I* can go to bed. She used to do stuff all the time with her old friends—work out at the gym, play tennis, go to gallery openings and parties and stuff. Now she only ever talks with them on the phone, and that's just once in a while.

Which leads me to number four, and the biggest whopper of all: Talking to a shrink will help us adjust to our new life.

Don't look at me—seeing Dr. Holkke once a week wasn't my idea. My opinion? If Dr. Holkke really wanted to help out, he'd lend us the money for a new set of front tires. Instead he's constantly asking me all these *How are you feeling?* and *What's on your mind today?* questions—stuff he couldn't care less about. What he's really trying to get me to talk about is my dad, which is, frankly: (a) none of his beeswax and (b) kind of a sore subject with me at the moment.

My parents split up a couple of months ago, just before the Fourth of July.

To Dr. Holkke, though, I just say stuff like "not bad" or "not much" and sit there for half an hour until it's time to switch places with Mom out in the waiting room. Which isn't much better, by the way, because Dr. Holkke doesn't have any decent magazines. I swear he thinks kids still like to read *Highlights*. Basically, the only thing good about the whole setup is that I get to leave school early on Wednesdays. But I *for sure* don't feel any better adjusted afterward. Neither does Mom. She may act all jolly and jokey when she comes out of Dr. Holkke's office, but her eyes are usually puffy. And if I ask her what's wrong in the car, she says something totally random like we should get a pizza for dinner.' Lie, lie, lie. One time I tried to call a spade a shovel. I said, "Maybe we should stop seeing Dr. Holkke if all he's going to do is nose around in our private life and make you cry." She laughed. She pulled my ear the way I hate but secretly sort of like. She said, "That's what he's supposed to do, Nicky. Talking to him makes me feel *better*."

Such a liar.

So when she says we'll give it a few days with Reggie—just to see how things work out—I know she's lying about that too. Reggie is here to stay. And I'm telling you right now, it's all going to end in tears.

SATURDAY MORNING. MY SO-CALLED BEDROOM.

I wake up and he's staring right at me.

Reggie, I mean. He's so close I can feel his breath on my face. His chin is literally resting on the edge of my pillow.

"Gross," I say. "You ever hear of mouthwash?"

He whines a little and licks his chops.

"Beat it," I say.

He doesn't. He just rolls those big, sad eyes.

"Go tell Mom if you've got to pee," I say. "You're hers, not mine."

I reach for the remote on the coffee table. I zap through the channels until I find a rerun of *Dr. Ice*, the one where he only pretends to be a bad guy so he can infiltrate the headquarters of the Heat. I get kind of wrapped up in the episode, even though I've already seen it ten hundred times. Until I hear Reggie by the front door whining again.

"Put a cork in it!" I say, looking over.

Oh great. He's standing in a big puddle of pee.

I climb out of the sofa bed. I tiptoe over to Mom's room and rap on her door.

Silence.

"Better wake up," I say. "Somebody had an accident, and it wasn't *me*."

Silence.

I press my ear to the door. Usually I can hear her snoring, which she says she doesn't do, but I know better. "Mom?" I say. Still nothing. I open the door and stick my head in, though, technically speaking, I'm not supposed to unless I'm invited. But I'm not taking any chances these days.

She's totally fine. Curled up like a little baby. Must be she has her earplugs in again. The car alarms are always going off in the alley behind our building.

I close the door without waking her. It's Saturday. She has the day off—the Ambulance Chasers are closed Saturday and Sunday even if their TV ads run all weekend—so she likes to sleep in. Fine by me. I make my own breakfast anyway. We would both rather have a bowl of Galactic Crunch than eggs and all that. Plus you don't have to be a rocket scientist to work a toaster. I like to eat right after I get up, and she usually needs a cup of black coffee to get things rolling. Then we do the laundry and grocery shopping at the strip mall, while every other kid in America gets to watch cartoons. Welcome to my fantastic new life.

Reggie scratches at the door and whimpers.

"*Shh*," I say. "You're already in the doghouse. That's a new carpet. The landlord's going to go mental."

I get the sponge mop from behind the kitchen door, run it under the faucet with some dishwashing liquid, and do my best to clean up Reggie's mess. We can't afford to lose our security deposit right now. Our front tires are, like, totally bald.

I crouch down to see if the wet spot smells. Reggie licks my face. It happens so fast, I can't do anything about it. One minute his big, pink tongue is in his mouth, and the next it's leaving a slime trail on my chin. "Gross!" I say. "Do that again and it's straight back to the pound with you." He looks exactly like he's going to do it again, so I head for the kitchen to stow the mop.

He makes a point of scratching the door again as soon as I get back.

"OK, OK," I say. "I'll take you out. But only this once. Then you need to work it out with your real master." I have a pee myself, then change out of my pj's. It takes me a few minutes to figure out how to hook Reggie's leash onto his collar. Thank God it's just the normal kind, not the seeing-eye kind, which, if you can believe what's on TV these days, looks like something a paratrooper would wear.

Reggie scrambles down the front stoop and makes a beeline for the nearest hydrant—dragging me behind. I don't even want to tell you what he does right there on the sidewalk in front of everybody. I yank on his leash, whisper to him to act natural, and just keep walking toward the end of Eden Street.

Don't look at me! Mom should totally have taken him out before she went to bed last night. It's not *my* fault she dragged him back from the pound instead of doing the grocery shopping. Plus I didn't think to bring anything to scoop it up with. What do I know about dogs? All I've ever had was a goldfish, which you can't even count as a pet. It's fun to watch goldfish for, like, five minutes, and then they just turn into another piece of furniture. Mine died after about a month. I swear I fed it every day. Supposedly they just don't live that long. They probably die of boredom. Dogs are a different story, though. Dogs are real pets. They have needs. The grown-ups in my old neighborhood were constantly taking their dogs out for walks. Scooping up stuff.

Reggie tugs at his leash when we reach the corner. He wants to keep going. I look back. The landlord's standing at the hydrant in his bathrobe, staring down at Reggie's mess. Oh great. I tell Reggie I'll take him as far as the monument, but that's it.

Bunker Hill Monument is one of the few places in Charlestown I know how to get to besides my new school. I'm not really supposed to be wandering around the neighborhood on my own. We don't exactly live in the best part of town—even though Mom keeps telling her friends it's perfectly safe. Colorful, she calls it. Transitional, which means nice houses are all jumbled up with sketchy ones that look like they might have been nice once but aren't anymore. Like ours.

Reggie sniffs the air, looking a little confused.

"It's a left," I tell him.

Reggie takes a left turn onto Main Street—so he must know his right from his left at least—and we hoof it past Walker, Franklin, Sullivan, and Salem, just like a regular kid out walking his dog. When we get to Austin, though, which is also the turnoff to Taco Mucho and the strip mall, Reggie suddenly seems to get his bearings. He totally picks up speed. It's all I can do to scramble after him by the time he barrels through the big intersection at Main and Warren. I try shouting, "Heel, boy!" but he obviously didn't learn that one in guide-dog school, because he takes Warren and just keeps dragging me along. Before you know it, we're at Monument Ave. "Take a left!" I shout.

He comes skidding to a halt.

"It's this left," I say, as soon as I catch my breath. He shoots me a look that says *please!* before taking another small step down Warren.

"Left, I said!"

Finally he does as he's told.

Monument Ave is pretty steep, so there's no question of running now. In fact we're both huffing and puffing by the time we get to the grassy square at the top. Supposedly the Bunker Hill Monument in the middle of the square marks the spot of a Revolutionary War battle where the Minutemen were told not to shoot any redcoats until they could see the whites of their eyes. Except that this hill isn't actually Bunker Hill. It's Breed's Hill. Bunker Hill is across Tremont Street, where they built a bunch of apartment buildings before they thought of putting up a monument. Anyway, the one on Breed's Hill looks like a giant granite toothpick.

Reggie heads straight for three old guys playing bocce. Before I know it, Reggie's got a red wooden ball in his mouth.

"Put that back!" I say.

He doesn't. He trots over to one of the old guys, dragging me behind. The man takes the ball. "Thanks, Reggie!" he says, patting him on the head and feeding him a treat out of his pocket. One of the two other old guys unhooks him from his leash. The third one points at the grass and tells him to fetch. Reggie heads back to get another ball.

I stand there like an idiot, not knowing what to do.

"Where's Old Alf?" the first old guy says when he notices me.

"Alf who?" I say.

"Alf Santorello," he says. "Reggie's master. Who are you?"

"Nicky," I say. "Who are you?"

"I'm Sal. That's Floyd," he says, pointing to the black guy on his left, "and this guy here is Mickey." He jerks his thumb at a guy with pointy ears who's holding Reggie's leash.

"So why's a young punk like you out walking Reggie?" Mickey says to me. "You didn't steal him, did you?"

"Of course not!" I say. As if!

"I hope Old Alf isn't sick," Sal says.

"He hasn't been by the monument in weeks," Floyd says.

They all start talking at once: Alf was perfectly fine the last time they saw him. He was the very picture of health—except, of course, for his blindness. But illnesses can suddenly attack you when you're their age. Accidents can happen. You never know . . .

I have no clue who this Alf Santorello is. But it obviously didn't work out between him and Reggie or Mom wouldn't have been able to get Reggie for free at the pound yesterday instead of taco fixings. It's true, he's not so good at taking orders—he seems to want to drag me off in the wrong direction at every corner—but I'm beginning to wonder if there's more to this whole guide-dog story than meets the eye.

Good thing I started keeping this mental log. I may have a real Dr. Ice–type detective case on my hands.

For now, though, I don't answer any of their questions. I just swipe the leash out of Mickey's hand and tell Reggie to *Come on, boy.* I don't need to say it twice. He's off like a shot, headed back down Monument Ave. All I can do is trot after him. When we get to the bottom of the hill, he tries to turn left onto Warren. Enough is enough. I shout, "Right!" He pretends he doesn't hear me. I shout "Right!" three more times—because that's the only way I know how to get back to Eden Street—but he keeps pulling me left. That does it! I yank on his leash with all my might and shout, "Stop!"

Reggie stops dead in his tracks like he's been zapped by one of the Heat's secret ray guns.

"Bad dog!" I shout. "Really bad dog!" I raise my hand, you know, to give him a little warning—show him who's boss.

He yelps. He ducks his head. He crouches with his tail between his legs. His ears go all flat and he starts shaking like a leaf.

I lower my hand then. I wasn't *really* going to hit him. It's just that he was making me so mad. I kneel next to him and he flinches. "It's OK," I say. "I won't hurt you." But he won't look me in the eye now. "Sorry," I say. I give his head a pat—just a little one—to make sure he understands I mean it. His ears perk back up. He sticks his tongue up my nose. Gross! I stand back up and tell him to watch it with that thing.

"Now go right!" I say.

Lo and behold, he actually does as he's told.

SATURDAY MORNING. BACK AT THE APARTMENT.

Mom's having a bowl of cereal in front of the TV when I finally get Reggie through the front door. "What did you spill on the rug?" Mom says. It's the very first thing out of her mouth. Not: *Hey, good morning, Nicky.* Not: *So where have you been?*

I tell her exactly who spilled what.

"Well, why didn't you let him out?" she says. "Now I'm going to have to get the carpet steam cleaned."

"He's your dog," I say.

"I got him for you," she says.

"*I* told you to take him back to the pound," I remind her.

She sighs. She turns to the TV without answering. In Littleton she barely ever watched television, except for a few British gardening shows on cable. Now the remote is permanently stuck to her hand. One of those talk shows is on, the kind where a bunch of ladies sit around and tell about how, just when it all looked hopeless, an angel made a miracle.

So it's going to be one of those days.

I head for the kitchen. Reggie follows me. I fix myself a bowl of Galactic Crunch. He watches my every move. I shove a big spoonful into my mouth. He licks his chops.

"You're barking up the wrong tree," I say.

He whines.

"She only bought one can of dog food last night, and you already ate it, pal," I say. "There's no telling when we'll get to the Supa-Sava today, now that she's in one of her moods. You should have stuck with that Alf Santorello dude."

I break down after a couple more spoonfuls and set my bowl on the floor. Reggie licks my hand, then slurps out what's left of the milk and soggy cereal.

"Are we doing shopping and laundry or what?" I shout into the living room.

"Right after this program," Mom calls back.

"What are you going to do with Reggie?" I say.

"Leave him here, I guess," she says.

I'm just about to say, "It's your security deposit," but I don't. Instead I go to the fridge to get a glass of fruit punch. I shouldn't really be getting involved, seeing how he's not my dog.

SATURDAY MORNING. IN THE CAR.

Mom and I are on the way back from the strip mall. We've worked out this routine where we wash all our clothes at the coin-op place next to Taco Mucho and then, while they're in the dryer, scoot across the parking lot to the Supa-Sava to do the weekly groceries. Since the clothes are usually dry by the time we're waiting in line at the register, I dash back to the coin-op to fold while Mom pays up and stows everything in the car's trunk. It's called killing two birds with one stone. Only trouble is: I never know what to do with all the time we've saved.

I flick on the car radio, expecting to get classical music. Bad seventies rock comes blasting out of every speaker. One of those hair bands starts screaming, *"We are the champions!"* over and over again. It's Mom's secret favorite AM station. Sometimes she likes to rock out to heavy metal when she's in the car alone, but she forgets to change the dial back. Don't look at me—I hadn't even been born yet.

"Let's go into the city," I say.

"We *are* in the city," Mom says. "Look at this traffic."

"I mean into Boston," I say, pointing at the skyscrapers.

"Now?" she says. "The milk will spoil."

"I mean after we put away the groceries," I say, trying not to roll my eyes.

"Some other time," she says. "It was a tough workweek."

Next it's a song about taking it to the streets. "I can't believe we live in America's most historic city," I say, "and I've never actually stepped foot in it."

"You have too," she says. "What about when you walked the Freedom Trail with your father last year? You must have seen everything worth seeing."

"That was practically two years ago," I say. "I barely remember a thing about it." Not true. It was a great day, and I remember every single detail. Dad and I took the commuter rail into North Station, walked all over Boston, had lunch at Quincy Market, rode the T—what everyone here calls the subway—and it was totally awesome because it was just the two of us.

"Has he called yet?" I say.

"I spoke to him at work yesterday," she answers.

"Which weekends does he want?"

"He didn't say."

Another lie?

I drop it for now. Like I say, it's a sore subject. I just stare out the window.

Mom switches the station to public radio, and there's a quiz show on. A few minutes later she says, "Is going into Boston today really important to you?"

"No," I say. "Whatever." We drive the rest of the way to Eden Street, pretending we're both guessing which three words in English, beginning with S and a vowel, make the sh sound.

"Let's do it," Mom says as she's squeezing into half a parking space a million miles from our building.

"Do what?" I say.

"Head into Boston. We'll go right after lunch."

"You sure?" I say.

"It'll do us both good to get out," she says.

"Cool," I say.

We decide as we're unloading the car and schlepping the groceries over to our stoop that we'll actually go *before* lunch—make a couple of tuna sandwiches and bring them along with us. Mom tells me, while she's fumbling with the keys to the front door, that there's a nice park called the Public Garden with a fake lake and swan boats where we can have a picnic. Swan boats? I tell her I'd rather take the duck boat tour all the kids in homeroom were talking about. Supposedly they go on both land and water. Mom says *We'll see, but that doesn't sound very safe.* She opens the front door.

And there's Reggie, lying in the middle of the room. He's barfed all over the place. It's green and slimy—just like the ooze that comes out of the back of Dr. Ice's escape-mobile—and floating on top are little pieces of what look like parsley. That's when I notice the poor philodendron. There's nothing left to it but a stem and chewed-up leaves.

Reggie moans.

Mom puts her hands on her hips, all mad.

"Don't look at me!" I say. "I warned you about leaving him here alone."

"Well, why didn't you feed him something before we left?" Mom says.

"What?" I say. "SpaghettiOs?"

Her face turns red, but she doesn't start yelling. Instead she sort of deflates, like a balloon you let all the air out of.

"What was I thinking, getting a dog?" she says. "The pound had plenty of cats."

I tell Mom to call 911. They put her on hold. I get the mop out of the kitchen and do my best with the carpet, while Reggie moans and barfs up the rest of what he ate. 911 tells Mom they don't make animal calls and gives her the number of the nearest vet. She dials it and gets put on hold again. In the meantime, I grab the red plastic dishpan from under the kitchen sink and hover it below Reggie's chin. When the vet finally comes on the line, Mom explains the situation. Mom says "Really?" and "Are you sure?" a couple of times and hangs up. Then she just stands there.

"Well?" I say.

"Look at that rug," she whispers.

"Well, what did the vet say?"

"He said philodendron leaves are toxic to dogs."

"Like deadly?" I say.

"We need to drive Reggie over there as soon as possible," she says. "Try and get him onto his feet. I'll go get the car."

"What about the groceries?" I say.

"Just shove the milk and whatever else will go bad into the fridge."

She turns and walks out the door.

As soon as I find Reggie's leash, I hook it onto his collar and say *Come on, boy.* He doesn't budge. I tell him *It's time to take a little ride downtown* and tug. Nothing. I tell him *Sorry, but this is for your own good* and yank the leash until I get him onto all fours. I drag him toward the door, saying more stupid stuff like: *Come on, boy* and *This way, boy* and *Let's go for a nice little ride, boy.* He finally follows me out of the apartment and down the front stoop, weaving like a drunken sailor. Mom has the car running curbside. She's left the back door wide open. I push Reggie onto the seat. He barfs up a few more chunks of philodendron and then passes out. I climb into the front. Mom hits the gas and we tear off down Eden Street.

"So where's the vet's office?" I say.

"Fairfield Street," she says.

"Where's that?" I say.

"I don't know," she says. She digs her work cell phone out of her pocketbook—the one we're never supposed to use for personal stuff—and tosses it to me. "You better call them back. Dial 411 and ask for Back Bay Animal Care."

The vet's receptionist tells me their office is at the corner of Fairfield and Commonwealth Ave. I ask her how to get there from Charlestown. She tells me we just need to head for the Public Garden. Commonwealth Avenue starts on the Arlington Street side. The rest is easy, she says, because all the cross streets in the Back Bay are alphabetical. We just need to drive up Comm Ave past the B, C, D, and E streets until we reach Fairfield.

I would think that's pretty cool if we weren't in such a hurry.

□□□

A couple of the vet's assistants lift Reggie out of the backseat and flop him onto a wheelie-bed. They take him around the back to where the emergency room is. The receptionist out front tells us to take a seat. We read stale magazines for I don't know how long before the vet finally comes out to talk to us.

"Reggie's going to be fine," he says. "I had to pump his stomach, though. So it'll be a couple of days before he's his old self."

I have no clue what Reggie's old self *was*.

"We were just getting back from the store with more dog food," Mom says. "He must have been a lot hungrier than we thought."

"Dogs don't eat house plants out of hunger," the vet says. "It's a way of acting out. Has your family been through any major changes lately?"

Where do I begin?

"We just got Reggie from the pound," I say, before Mom can start blabbing all our personal business to total strangers.

"That probably explains it," the vet says. "Give him lots of water. No dry dog food for a week, just canned. But only feed him half a can twice a day. He looks a little overweight. Keep those houseplants out of reach, and try to make Reggie feel as welcome and safe as possible. He's probably been through a lot recently."

Mom nods. I nod. What else can we do?

The vet tells Mom she can settle up with the receptionist—they take most major credit cards. She asks him how much it's going to be. She literally gasps when the vet tells her. We watch him head back into the ER.

"I should have gotten you another goldfish," Mom says, standing.

SUNDAY MORNING. EDEN STREET.

I'm stepping out for a little fresh air," I say. Mom's doing the crossword on the sofa. Without looking up, she does her usual *Don't go too far* and *Be careful out there*. I check up on Reggie on my way out. We've made a bed of old quilts for him near the front door. He's just lying there, staring at the same TV news program Mom isn't watching either. He hasn't really moved since we brought him back from the vet. He hasn't touched any of the expensive dog food we put in his new dish. Maybe the vet was right: Maybe he's depressed about ending up in a place he never wanted to be, living with a couple of strangers who totally don't get him.

I grab Reggie's new matching water bowl and freshen it up with water from the bathroom sink. He gives it a sniff when I set it in front of him, then settles his chin back onto his paws. He doesn't even try to lick my hand or wag thank you.

"I'm going now," I say. "See you in a little while."

Silence.

I make sure to let the screen door slam a little on the way out.

The landlord shouts out his front window for us to take it easy; he can hear every move we make up there. "Was that you I saw with a shepherd the other day?" he says. "Your mother asked me about a dog, not a horse."

I give him one of those *Can't talk now, gotta run!* waves and head straight for the Bunker Hill Monument.

I'm in luck. Those old guys are playing bocce, just like the last time.

"You're back," the one named Sal says.

I shrug.

"Where's Reggie today?" says the one named Mickey, who looks like an elf. "You didn't sell him, did you?"

"He's at home," I say. "He's not feeling so hot."

"Not his hip again!" Floyd says.

"Upset stomach," I say.

"What did you say your name was?" Sal says.

"Nicky."

"The boy must be Alf Santorello's grandson," Floyd says. "From that daughter of his in California."

I don't say yes or no.

"Well, *that* explains it," Sal says.

Floyd and Mickey chuckle to themselves and slap each other's backs. The boy's just visiting his old granddad, they say—that explains it.

"So how do *you guys* know Alf?" I say. Which is the actual reason for me coming all the way back up here. I'm trying to find out, if I can, why Reggie is so depressed. I'm thinking maybe it's because he feels bad about whatever he did that got him fired from his job with this Alf Santorello dude. It must have been something pretty bad—worse than snarfing down an entire philodendron—to land him in the pound.

"VFW," Sal says, jerking his thumb in the direction of a big brick building across the square. "We were in the same platoon with Old Alf in Korea. Us three here live at the home for vets back there."

"Your granddad used to walk Reggie over here from the North End most afternoons," Floyd says.

Aha! So Reggie comes from the North End, wherever that is.

"Old Alf'd bowl a few games with us, then head home," Mickey says.

"Wait a sec," I say. "How'd he do that, if he's, you know, *blind*?"

Sal cups his ear. Floyd sniffs the air. Mickey licks his finger and raises it to the wind. They all laugh.

"He's a better bocce player than Mickey here," Sal says.

"Is not," Mickey says. "We're about even."

"But we haven't seen him in weeks," Sal says.

"We were getting worried," Floyd says. "What with Alf living in that big old house by himself. We were even thinking of dropping in on him one of these days."

"Except none of us drives anymore," says Sal. "And walking across the bridge, like your granddad used to do, is out of the question."

"Bum knee," Mickey says, slapping his thigh.

"Bad ticker," Floyd says, tapping his chest.

"So why don't Old Alf come to Charlestown with you?" Mickey says. "Don't he like us still?"

Obviously, they don't know any more about what happened between Alf Santorello and Reggie than I do. If I want to find out, I'm going to have to make a little trip over to the North End and have a chat with this Old Alf in person.

"I'll tell him you asked, next time I see him," I say. I make a big show out of looking at my watch. "Yikes, I gotta get going," I say, turning back toward Monument Ave.

"Tell your granddad we still need a fourth for our game," Mickey calls after me. "Tell him it's more fun with partners."

"Tell him Mickey cheats like crazy when we play cutthroat," Floyd adds.

All three of them bust a gut laughing.

"See you guys around," I say.

"We'll be here," Sal says, winking.

SUNDAY NIGHT. BACK AT THE APARTMENT—WHERE ELSE?

Will you put that thing away?" Mom says.

I'm playing one of my video games on the TV while she sits at the dining table, paying a bunch of bills. Typical

Sunday-night behavior for both of us. "But I'm just about to win," I say.

"All that beeping and booping is driving me crazy," she says. Obviously the checkbook isn't balancing again. She keeps punching numbers into the calculator, shaking her head, and sighing.

"How about five more minutes?" I say.

"Do you have to argue with me about everything?" she says.

Over in the corner, Reggie pricks up his ears.

I shut off the video game. I wasn't that close to winning anyway—not really. I grab the remote and channel surf, trying to find something that isn't a bunch of grown-ups voting each other off an island. Suddenly I come across this show about the Korean War. Well, actually, it's mostly about a gang of army doctors who drink lots of martinis and play practical jokes on each other, when they're not stitching soldiers up and sending them back to the front.

"Nicholas!" Mom says, slamming her pen down on the table.

(See, I told you: She only calls me Nicholas when she's mad . . .)

"What?" I say. "This is educational."

"It's just as bad as the video games—a lot of blood and gore passed off as entertainment. Can't you read a book?"

"You never cared about the video games when I had my own room," I say.

"I *did* care!" she says—practically yelling. "I've always hated those stupid things. I just bit my tongue. Believe me, if I'd had *my* way about it, they would never have been allowed in the house."

I shut off the TV. I just sit there. I don't want to read a book.

"We're going to have to cut down on all this eating out and takeout," she says. "Our budget just can't handle it."

I don't even go there.

"A stomach pump!" she says, shaking the checkbook at me. "That was our new set of tires."

Reggie must know she's talking about him. He hoists himself up and wanders over to where I'm sitting on the couch. He puts his paw on my knee and cocks his head. He gives me this funny *What's going on?* look. You can practically see the cartoon question mark over his head, which makes me smile. He must be feeling a little better today, because he's licked his food and water bowls clean. I scratch him behind the ears. Supposedly dogs like that.

"Don't let him up on the couch!" Mom says. "He'll shred the fabric with those toenails. He's already cost enough money this week—not to mention a steam cleaning, eventually."

Money, money, money. Back in Littleton we never worried about money.

I tell Reggie to sit. He takes his paw away and sits at my feet. I pat his back and scratch his neck until Mom finally puts the checkbook and calculator away. "That's it," she says. "I give up on this day." She closes herself into her room without washing her face or brushing her teeth—two things she always makes me do.

I wait a few minutes, till I see the light go out through the crack in her door.

Then I pat the sofa cushion next to me.

Reggie leaps up in a single bound.

MONDAY MORNING.
THE LIVING ROOM.

I wake with Reggie still lying at my feet on the sofa. When I sit up, his tail starts to thump. Today he seems to be as good as new. So that stomach pump must have worked, even if it did cost as much as a new set of tires. I look around, waiting for Mom to yell at me about his toenails. But the coast is clear. She must have already left for work— the ironing board's out, her makeup's all over the dining table, and what's left of her morning coffee is scorching in the automatic drip machine.

I reach for the remote and flick on the TV. I'm kind of addicted right now to this psychic on one of the cable channels who claims he can communicate by mental telepathy with the pets of the people in his audience. By the first commercial break, though, my stomach's growling. I get the box of Galactic Crunch from the kitchen and eat handfuls out of the box. Breakfast in bed. I offer Reggie some—even though the vet said no dry dog food—which makes his tail thump even harder. Some lady's parrot has stopped talking to her. The psychic tells the lady her bird is mad about all the peanuts she feeds him because they give him indigestion. The lady promises to give him more fruit and suddenly I'm running late for homeroom—again. I throw on some school clothes, fold up the sofa, and drag Reggie out for a pee. When we get back, I fix him half a can of dog food and fill up his water bowl.

Yikes, am I ever late!

The school yard is pretty empty by the time I come chugging through the gates. In fact there's only one other kid on the playground, a girl leaning against the front door talking on her cell phone. (Playground my foot. It's more like a parking lot with a couple of swing sets.) She ends her call when she sees me. "Hi," she says. "You're the new kid in Gilmore's homeroom."

"So?" I say.

"We're in the same grade," she says. "But I'm in McClafferty's homeroom."

"Which we're both late for," I say, motioning for her to step aside.

"I'm cool," she says. "My mom's a nurse. She works the night shift Sundays and Thursdays, which means I have to look after my little brothers until she gets home in the morning." She holds up her cell phone like it's some sort of proof. It has stupid pink puppy stickers all over it. "That was her just now," she says, "wondering what I did with the *niño*'s other bib."

"And your point is—?" I say. Marky, my best friend back in Littleton, warned me this would happen. He told me to find a couple of cool kids to hang out with ASAP. Otherwise, he said, all the losers would come after me. According to Marky, the losers always try to make friends with the new kid first, hoping that, by the time you discover everyone in school hates them, it's too late because now you've been branded a loser too. Marky should know. He's had to move around a lot because his dad's a major in the army. He'd already lived in something like five or six states besides Massachusetts before I'd ever even met him.

"My *point* is, I'm not technically late," Rita says. "I've worked it all out with McClafferty. She turns a blind eye on Mondays and Fridays, especially since I'm so ridiculously far ahead of everyone else in her lame-o math class."

"Yeah, well, I *am* late, so if you don't mind—"

She holds out her hand. "Rita de la Cruz," she says with a for-real Spanish accent. "I didn't catch your name."

She must be Latino. I take Spanish fourth period. But I still don't get why they don't call Italians Latinos, since Rome—where they *actually* spoke Latin—is in Italy, not Spain. Besides which, Latin America isn't even on the same continent as Spain.

"Um, I kind of need to get inside," I say.

Rita makes a big show out of pulling the door open

for me, like she's the lovely game show assistant revealing what's behind curtain number three—which is an empty hallway of beat-up lockers. I step inside and make a dash for Mr. Gilmore's classroom. Rita isn't all that easy to shake. She follows right behind, her clogs clacking against the linoleum. "What time's your lunch recess, bro?" she says. "Maybe we can grab a bite together."

But it's too late to answer, thank God. I'm at homeroom.

MONDAY MORNING. HOMEROOM.

Glad you decided to hang with us today, Nicky," Mr. Gilmore says. He's already reading the announcements when I wrestle the door open. (It's an old, crappy school, like I said, and the classroom doors weigh about a thousand pounds each and totally stick.) I don't say anything back. I've already used up every excuse in the book. I just take my seat and try to ignore the fact that everyone is staring at me.

First period: math. My most unfavorite subject. At my old school in Littleton, all our classes were divided into three tracks—Pegasus, Orion, and Phoenix—because, supposedly, we were all stars, even though everybody knew the track names were just code for Smart, Average, and Dumb. Here in Charlestown, there's only one track. And believe me, it ain't the fast one.

Gilmore stands at the board, explaining how decimal

points work and how easy it is to move them backward and forward in your head when you're multiplying or dividing by ten. He tries to act all cool, cracking jokes and talking like he's from the hood. But it couldn't be more obvious that he's from the suburbs and fresh out of teachers' college. The Townies in homeroom—that's what they call tough white kids from Charlestown—totally eat Gilmore for breakfast. Anyway, we covered decimals last year back in Littleton. So I give myself permission to worry about something else. Like the fact it couldn't be any clearer that *I'm* from the suburbs.

I try to assess my own chances with the Townies. Marky says the bullies always go after the new kids too. You have to establish some street cred with them right away or you're hosed. The Townie leader of sixth grade is Timmy Burns, who happens to be in my homeroom. He roves around with Johnny Hedges and Chris McDuff and a couple of other sidekicks. Whenever Timmy says something, everyone laughs like it's the most hilarious thing in the entire universe. Personally, I don't see what's so great about him. Back in my old school he would never be popular. The popular kids in Littleton weren't bullies. They just had serious money.

I sneak a quick look over my shoulder. Timmy Burns is staring right at me. Before I can pretend to be looking somewhere else—out the window, maybe—he gives me the finger. Oh great.

"Earth to Nicky," Gilmore says from up front. "The blackboard is this way."

I turn around, and everybody laughs.

"Sorry," I say. "I was paying attention, I swear."

"Oh yeah?" Gilmore says. "Then why don't *you* tell us where the decimal point goes when you divide this numeral by ten thousand."

I have a quick look at the blackboard. "At the front. But first you need to add two zeros."

"You're right," Gilmore says, frowning.

"Brownnose," Timmy Burns singsongs from behind me. Everybody laughs.

"I'd really appreciate it if you and Timmy would save your socializing until recess," Gilmore says. He turns to the blackboard to write out another equation.

A second later, a spitball hits the back of my neck. I don't look around. It's pretty obvious where it came from.

"Hey, Brownie," Timmy Burns hisses. "No brownnoses allowed in Chucktown."

I just pretend I'm deaf. But I can totally feel myself going red. We had brownies back in Littleton. They were always waving their hands around, trying to answer all the questions to prove to everybody how smart they were. I'm definitely not a brownie. I'm not even that smart. I try not to sigh. This just isn't going to be my day. Mondays, man. I'm telling you.

◼◼◼

MONDAY AFTERNOON.
OUT ON EDEN STREET.

I let Reggie out to do his business as soon as I'm back from school. Walking him has obviously become my job even though, technically speaking, he belongs to Mom. But she doesn't get home from the Ambulance Chasers for another two hours, and I can't very well let him have another accident. The landlord's already cheesed off about Reggie's size. The last thing I need right now is for him to hear Reggie scratching at the door and decide it's time to check on his new carpet before we get it steam cleaned.

Reggie and I head straight for the monument.

The old guys all wave hello. They make a big fuss over Reggie, like they haven't seen him in a million years. I tell them to go easy with the dog treats since his stomach is still a little iffy.

"So how's your granddad?" Sal says.

"Oh fine," I say.

They've gotten it into their heads that Alf Santorello is my granddad. Don't look at me—it was Floyd who came up with the idea. I'm just going with the flow, which is a heck of a lot easier than explaining how I actually ended up in Charlestown walking an ex-seeing-eye dog that isn't even mine.

"So what did you guys *do* in Korea, anyway?" I say. I'm pretending to shoot the breeze with them while they play bocce and Reggie fetches balls, but what I'm actually doing is pumping them for more information about where I can find Old Alf in the North End—as soon as we get a chance to sneak over there. "Did you mostly sit around in a tent drinking martinis and playing practical jokes, like on TV?"

Man does that set them off!

I get an earful about long marches in the rain, trench foot, wormy food rations, and watching their best buddies go down all around them in surprise attacks by the Chinese. I also learn that Sal and Alf grew up in the North End of Boston, where the Italian families lived, that Floyd grew up in the South End, where the blacks lived, and that Mickey grew up right here in Charlestown, where the Irish lived. Sal says they all got thrown together into the same platoon when they got drafted, even though Boston was segregated at the time, and that they would never have met each other otherwise. They tell me that Alf Santorello lost his eyesight during the Battle of Pork Chop Hill, when a mortar shell exploded next to him and shrapnel flew into his eyes. The army shipped him home, and the VA—whatever that is—retrained him to be a dispatcher for a cab company. According to Sal, Old Alf's been living in the house where he grew up in the North End ever since. Unfortunately, I can't ask *where* in the North End because, supposedly, I'm staying with him there.

I tell the old guys I'd better be getting a move on.

At the bottom of Monument Ave, Reggie tries as usual

to go left instead of right. I check my watch. Mom will be getting back from the Ambulance Chasers soon. She'll go mental if I'm not there. But I can't resist. I'm dying to know where else in the neighborhood Reggie would lead me if he were out on an afternoon walk with Old Alf instead of me.

So I let Reggie turn left.

We hoof it down Warren past a bunch of stores and a really old-looking tavern until we take a right onto Park, which dumps us back out on Main Street at City Square. Directly in front of us is an old iron bridge that crosses the Charles River. On the opposite side, there's a bunch of brick buildings. To the right, there's a brand-new park. Beyond it is downtown and Boston Garden, which isn't a plant store like it sounds but a gigantic stadium. (I've actually been there, to see the All-Star Wrestling Extravaganza. But that's a story for another time.) On the left, the Charles opens out into a fancy boat marina. Reggie is all raring to take the footpath across the bridge—to the North End?—but I pull back hard on his leash. The sun is starting to set now, and if we don't get back to Eden Street ASAP, we'll both get grounded.

"Hey, kid!" somebody shouts. "Hey, you with the dog! Hold up!"

A bunch of teenagers are coming toward me from the park. I pretend I don't hear them and steer Reggie in the direction of Main Street—the nearest getaway—which must eventually end up back at Eden Street.

"I said hang on a second!"

I stop and wait for the teenagers to catch up. Reggie gives me an anxious little whine and tugs at his leash. But I have to stand my ground. It'll be much worse if I run. Reggie hugs my leg. I give his head a little pat. I should never have let him take that left at Monument Ave.

"You got a cigarette, kid?" one of the teenagers says. He looks just like Timmy Burns, only older. Maybe it's Timmy's Townie brother.

"I don't smoke," I say.

I can feel Reggie's whole body tensing up. The hair on the back of his neck starts to bristle.

"Got any money for cigarettes?" the Townie says, getting right up in my face.

Reggie lets off this low, warning growl.

The guy steps back. "Whoa," he says. "Nice doggy."

Reggie bares his teeth. This time his growl means business.

"He's my guard dog," I say. "He's trained to protect me to the death."

"His or mine?" the guy says.

"That's your call," I say.

Reggie half barks, half snaps at the guy.

The Townie takes another step back. "You have a safe walk home now," he says.

The teens all back away and start laughing.

"Nice bluff," I whisper to Reggie, scratching him behind the ears.

He licks my hand.

"Home, boy," I say. He may be a lousy guide dog, but I've got to admit, he actually *is* a pretty good guard dog—even if he isn't mine, technically speaking. "Let's just keep this between you and me," I say.

But of course Reggie won't say anything to Mom. He's just a dog.

MONDAY NIGHT. BACK AT THE APARTMENT.

Not even a whiff of supper cooking. Again.

"We're back," I say, unhooking Reggie's leash.

No answer.

I wander over to the sofa, where Mom is parked in front of the TV. "We're back," I say again. "Sorry it's almost dark."

"Oh good," she says, without even looking over. Instead she takes a sip of vino.

Glass half full or half empty?

"I'm hungry," I say.

"Takeout menus are on the coffee table," she says. "Order whatever you want. I'm kind of wrapped up in this." It's some eighties rerun about really rich people who live in a gigantic house with nothing better to do all day than be mean to each other. At the moment, two ladies wearing too much makeup are rolling around on the floor trying to tear each other's hair out.

I take Reggie's bowl into the kitchen and fix him what's

left from the can of dog food I opened this morning. For some reason, Mom only ever buys one can at a time. I set his bowl on the floor and watch him eat.

"Bring the bottle of wine with you when you come back!" Mom calls from the living room. "It's in the door of the fridge."

Obviously.

I reach for the phone on the wall. I know the number of the pizza place in the strip mall by heart. But I don't dial it. Instead I pretend to dial 911. "You gotta help me," I say to the dial tone. "I can't take it anymore! This apartment totally sucks and I don't even have my own room. Plus there's never any food in the house. Plus she's driving me crazy with all this moping around!" But then I feel kind of stupid and hang up. This time I dial the pizza place for real and order the usual: a large pie with half pepperoni and extra cheese, half veggie-the-works-no-olives. I pour myself a glass of fruit punch from the pitcher I've always got going in the fridge and head back into the living room. Reggie's so into his food he doesn't even look up.

I take a seat on the sofa next to Mom.

"Where's the wine?" she says.

"Oops," I say.

"Who were you talking to in there?" she says.

"Pizza guy," I say.

"No, before that," she says. "You were on the phone with somebody."

HOW I, NICKY FLYNN, FINALLY GET A LIFE (AND A DOG)

Oh great. I can't get her to pay attention to me for love nor money when I'm actually in the same room. But as soon as I get a little privacy, she's got better ears than Reggie. "You must have heard the landlord downstairs," I say, shrugging. "You know how thin these walls are."

She frowns.

"You reserve that steam cleaner yet?" I say.

She shrugs, a total grown-up kind of answer.

I sip my fruit punch. She drains her wineglass.

Soon a new show starts. This one's about a detective who has to go undercover and assume the identity of a missing business tycoon's dead twin brother to figure out what happened. It gets me thinking: What if I *kept* pretending to be Old Alf's grandson—just for a little while—to solve the mystery of how Reggie ended up at the pound? Maybe it wasn't Reggie's fault after all. I mean, let's face it: Old Alf is the one who seems to have just up and disappeared, not Reggie. Tell me there isn't something fishy about *that*. Besides, I'm already keeping a Dr. Ice mental log of Mom's criminal activity—and I'm not getting anywhere on that front. So I may as well see if I can crack this case at the same time. Plus I haven't got anything better to do.

At the next commercial, Mom grabs the remote to switch the channel.

"Hey, I was watching that," I say.

"This show's way too mature for you," she says. "When he's not killing people, he's making out with them."

"He also solves crimes," I say.

"Do your homework," she says.

"I don't have any," I say.

"Of course you do," she says. "You're in junior high. You must have some reading to do for English or something."

"I already read the book we're doing for English period *last* year."

"Did you tell your teacher that?"

"What for?" I say. "He's got, like, thirty other kids to worry about—all of them reading below grade level. Besides, I bet he couldn't pick me out of a lineup of ten sixth graders."

She gives me this weird look, like she's just waking up from a nap.

"I thought you liked your new school," she says.

"Are you *kidding*?" I say. "You have to pass through a freaking metal detector to get into the building."

"It's not that bad," she says.

"Whatever you say," I say. But she's right: I *am* exaggerating—a little.

We both go back to watching the detective show until the pizza guy finally rings the doorbell. "Don't forget my wine," Mom says. Which means I'm answering the door, I guess. I grab Mom's wallet out of her purse and pay the pizza guy, making sure to tip him a couple of bucks like you're supposed to. I bring the box and the jug of wine from the fridge into the living room and set them on the coffee table. We don't usually bother with plates on pizza night. We just eat out of the box, and shove whatever's leftover into the fridge. No fuss, no mess. We even keep a roll of paper towels next to the TV because it works better with greasy fingers than napkins.

I bite into my first slice—I'm starving—but Mom doesn't touch her side, which is veggie-the-works. She just tops up her glass and stares at me.

"What?" I say. "I swear I told them no olives. You can pick them off."

"Is your school really that bad?" she says, taking a sip.

"It's pretty bad," I say. I finish my slice and take another before the pizza gets cold.

"But you like living in Boston, right?" she says.

"We live in Charlestown," I say. "Boston's over there."

"We couldn't afford Back Bay or Beacon Hill. You know that. The rents were ridiculous."

"We could if you'd just let Grandpa pay the rent," I say. "He told you he'd be happy to help out with a decent-size two-bedroom." Oops. I'm not supposed to know that. It just slipped out.

"That was a private conversation!" Mom says. "Were you eavesdropping again?"

"I couldn't help it!" I say. "We're never more than ten feet from each other in this place."

Mom takes a slice of pizza and begins picking the olives off it.

"I need you to try and understand how important it is for me to do this on my own," Mom says. "Without Grandpa's help, or anybody else's."

"Well, what do you do with the money Dad gives you every month?" I say.

She stops olive plucking to give me a good, long stare.

"Were you speaking with your father just now?" she says. "In the kitchen?"

"No."

"Are you sure?" she says.

One of the *S* words that makes a *sh* sound.

"I don't even have his new number!" I say. "You haven't let me speak to him since we moved here."

"That's not true!"

"It's been at least three weeks."

"I can't help it if he only ever calls me at work!" she says.

I scoop up my half of the pizza and stomp into the kitchen, slamming the door behind me, which causes the landlord to rap on his ceiling. Reggie, who's standing over by the fridge, has this really concerned look on his face, one that would make me laugh if I wasn't so mad. I see that he's licked his dish totally clean. So I offer him a slice of pizza. "It's OK," I say. "Everything's under control." Reggie takes the slice, keeping one eye on me. I set the rest of my half on the counter and tell Reggie to shove over. I hunker down next to him on the warm linoleum. He sticks his tongue in my ear. I tell him to quit it. He does it again, and I scratch his neck while he laps the grease off his paws and gets back to work on his slice.

"It's true, though," I say. Reggie looks up. "About not knowing Dad's new number. Or his new address. It's pretty obvious Mom doesn't want Dad to call me here at the apartment. The only reason I know he finally checked out of that motel and moved into a real apartment somewhere in Littleton is because I overheard her telling one of her friends that on the phone."

Reggie licks my hand.

I try to calm myself the way I usually do—by pretending to pack my knapsack with everything I'll need: Swiss Army knife, flashlight, rain poncho, deck of cards.

Pretty soon my thoughts drift to what I'll say to Mom when she follows me in here to make up. I hoist myself off the linoleum and add DOG FOOD in magic marker to the magnetized memo board on the fridge, where we write the weekly grocery list. I underline it three times.

TUESDAY, LUNCH RECESS. MY CRAPPY MIDDLE SCHOOL.

I sit in an empty swing on the playground—otherwise known as the school parking lot—to eat my sandwich. There's no big surprise waiting for me when I open the paper bag, since I make my lunch myself: a peanut butter and jelly with potato chips crunched on top, an individually wrapped stick of beef jerky, a single-serving thingy of chocolate pudding, and a box of fruit punch. All the basic food groups. My old school in Littleton had a cafeteria, and I got the hot lunch every day. But here there's only a lunchroom, which is basically the basement with fold-up tables. So you have to bring your own food. That's why, if the weather's decent, they let us eat in the yard.

I watch a bunch of the boys from my homeroom play kickball. Timmy Burns is the pitcher for the Townie team. He's pretty good, I have to admit. He gets a lot of people to pop out. He must put some sort of spin on the ball. We used to play kickball at my old school too. I was really good. Well, pretty good. I never got picked last when we were choosing up sides.

"Yo, bro!"

I turn around. Oh great. It's Rita, that girl with the pink puppy cell phone.

"I thought that was you," Rita says, plunking herself down in the next swing over. "What's shaking, dude?"

I shrug and take a bite out of my sandwich.

"PB and J?" she says. "Classic! I'm packing tuna fish today. South of the Border–style. I make it with jalapeños. Want to trade halfsies?"

"Just how Latino are you?" I say.

"Latina," she says. "I was born, like, three blocks from here. How about you?"

"Irish, mostly."

"No, I mean where're you from?"

"Littleton."

"Ooh, check you out," she says. "What's a rich kid from the suburbs doing this far downtown?"

"We're definitely not rich," I say. "It's a long story."

"Lay it on me," she says, taking a big bite of tuna.

Someone pops a foul ball in our direction. Rita leaps out of her swing and shoves her sandwich into my lap. She makes a dive for the ball and catches it just before it lands in the sandbox. Dirt goes flying everywhere. We all stare at her. The skirt she's wearing bunches up around her waist and you can totally see her underpants, which have ladybugs all over them. She's not even that embarrassed when she stands up and tugs it all down. She just tosses the ball back to Timmy and says, "How about letting me and my friend in on the game?"

"No girls allowed," he says. "Townie rules."

"That's *so* old-school," Rita says. "And hello! Instant replay? Did you not see the major-league save I just made, like, two seconds ago?"

"Buzz off, Ladybug. Go play with your boyfriend Brownie," Timmy says. Everyone laughs.

It's all I can do to keep myself from standing up and shouting: *I'm not a brownnose! And she's not my girlfriend! I don't even know her! I'm just an innocent bystander!* But that would make me look even more like a freak.

"Your loss," Rita says, shrugging. "I'll just let you get

back to playing with *your* boyfriends." She turns and comes trotting back to the swing set, wiping the sand off her knees.

"I can't believe you just did that," I say.

"Aw, that was nothing," she says. "You should see me at Ultimate Frisbee."

I stand. I hand her back her sandwich.

"Brownie, huh?" Rita says. "Cool name for a blond kid. That short for something?"

I head for the main doors.

Where the heck is that recess bell when you need it?

TUESDAY, FINAL BELL. HOMEROOM.

Mr. Gilmore tells me he'd like me to hang back at my desk for a few minutes so we can have a little chat. I sit down while everybody else packs up their English books and things. No doubt he's going to chew me out about showing up late for homeroom the second day in a row. Timmy Burns passes by on my left. "You're hosed now, Brownie," he says, punching me really hard in the arm. Oh great. It's official. The most popular guy in school now hates me.

I watch Gilmore erase the rest of the chalkboard. He's taking his sweet time—the usual teacher power-trip stuff. Finally he strolls over, jingling the change in his pockets. He sits on top of the desk in front of mine, all casual, as if he just wants to shoot the breeze.

I wait for him to get to the point.

"You're a very bright young man, Nicky," Gilmore says.

This throws me for a loop. I was expecting him to make me do lines on the blackboard, something like: *I promise never to be late for homeroom ever again.* "I wasn't that smart at my old school," I say.

He laughs. He asks me where I'm from. I tell him. He nods, probably thinking: *Rich kid*, just like Rita. "You must be really bored here," he says.

Of course I'm bored! Alert the media! As if school isn't *supposed* to be boring. "Oh, I'm OK," I say.

"Listen," he says, "I thought about moving you ahead a grade. But I decided against that. You've already had to make a whole new group of friends this year because of your big move."

Why do grown-ups always think kids make, like, instant friends?

"It's cool by me if you want to skip ahead in your math book," he says. "But that's not going to solve the fact that you've already read the novel we're doing in English."

So that's it. Mom ratted me out. I should have guessed ol' Gilmore didn't put two and two together on his own.

"It would be better if you waited for your classmates to catch up to you," he says. "That way you can all read together as a group. When it comes to English, discussion is an important part of the learning process."

"Yeah well, sitting around and staring out the window is

pretty much what's *making* me bored," I say. Why not call a spade a shovel here, as long as Gilmore brought it up?

Gilmore laughs again. "That's not what I meant," he says. "Maybe you could work on an independent study project during English period—just for the next couple of weeks or so."

"What's that?" I say.

"A book report," he says, "only more in-depth."

He tells me I could pick a topic that interests me, research it in the library, take lots of notes, and then write a paper on it. The project could be about anything I want.

"Anything?" I say.

"Sure," he says. "Got something in mind?"

"Maybe."

"Like what?"

"Seeing-eye dogs," I say, all casual. May as well get a little work done on my detective case, right? Two birds, one stone.

"Oh," he says. He looks confused, like I was supposed to say baseball or race cars or something.

"You know, like how they get trained," I say, "what they do all day, why most of them are German shepherds, why some of them end up getting fired by their masters—stuff like that."

"Oh," he says. "OK, Nicky. Write me a ten-page report on the life of seeing-eye dogs. I'll make you out a pass tomorrow afternoon so you can start spending English period in the library doing the research. That OK with you?"

"No," I say.

"Why not?" he says.

"Tomorrow's Wednesday. I always take off early on Wednesdays on account of—you know—my weekly appointment."

"That's right," he says. "I forgot. Thursday, then."

He waits for me to say something else, but I don't know what, so I tell him I better get going. He says fine, he'll see me tomorrow. I pack up my knapsack and get the heck out of there before he changes his mind.

LATER TUESDAY AFTERNOON. CHARLESTOWN BRIDGE.

Reggie and I are standing at the edge of the footpath that crosses the bridge to the North End. We've skipped visiting with the old guys today. Instead of heading up to Monument Square, we've made a beeline straight here so there's plenty of time to do a little sleuthing before dark.

"It's OK, boy," I say. "Show me where you'd normally go if I were Old Alf and you were on duty."

As usual, he doesn't need to be asked twice.

As soon as we step off the other side of the bridge, Reggie takes a left onto Commercial, then a quick right onto Prince. He knows exactly where he's going. It's a good thing too, because I wouldn't have a clue. Especially since, so far, the

North End looks exactly like Charlestown—grungy red-brick town houses with high stoops—except that all the storefronts seem to be Italian restaurants instead of Irish pubs. Reggie takes a sharp right at Hanover Street. There's a lot more hustle and bustle here. I wonder if Mom knows about this part of town. It's got a really cool mix of bakeries and shops. We pass a café where little old ladies are out front playing dominoes. We pass a health food store and a bookshop and a yoga studio—all the kinds of places Mom used to like to go to. Reggie stops outside Strazzulo's, an old-fashioned butcher shop with big links of sausage and gross dead rabbits hanging in the window. Reggie scratches at the door until the woman behind the counter comes and opens it for him. He walks straight inside like he owns the place. I follow along—what else can I do?—and stand beside him at the meat counter. The woman fetches a small, oily package out of the glass case and hands it to me. "I was just about to throw this out," she says. "You running errands for Mr. Santorello now?"

I nod. "I'm his grandson," I say. I can't believe how easy the words come sliding out of my mouth.

"That's a nice boy," she says. "I heard all about your poor nono's accident—how he fell right outside his house and broke his ankle."

Aha! No wonder Old Alf hasn't been walking across the bridge to the monument. It's my first real break in the case. I try my best to play it cool, though. I say, "It was a shock to everybody."

"You got a name?" she says.

"Nicky."

"You got a list?"

I shake my head no.

"Didn't he tell you what he wants?" she says.

I shake my head no again.

"Just stopping by to pick up Reggie's bones, eh?" she says. "Good. They seem to be working. He's not limping today. You got to watch those hips with shepherds, I keep telling your nono. Shepherds need plenty of calcium, I tell him. Let him know Mrs. Strazzulo's got some nice cutlets in this week. Tell him I can put it on account for him, if he's worried about you carrying around a lot of money."

I nod and tug at Reggie's leash. He's out the door like a shot, thank God. In fact, I barely have time to wave good-bye to Mrs. Strazzulo, let alone buy cutlets off her. We continue hoofing it down Hanover Street, past a used record shop and a post office and a hardware store. Next Reggie hangs a right onto Parmenter Street. It's a little more quiet here, with lots of pretty old town houses in better shape than on Prince Street. At Bartlett Place, Reggie leads me over to a stoop, where there's a lady about Mom's age tending to a window box of asters. Supposedly the flowers are called that because of their star shape. You know, like asterisk—that little star on keyboards and cell phones? Mom used to plant asters in the fall too. Asters and mums and I don't remember what all else. I told her at the Supa-Sava the other day that she should get a window box for the apartment. They had them on sale. She just said, *Yeah, maybe.* She won't do it, though. Not after what happened with the philodendron.

"How's my favorite neighborhood dog?" the lady calls over to Reggie. But she doesn't come over to pet him, which is what *I* would do if he were my favorite neighborhood dog. Maybe it's because she's surprised to see me at the other end of the leash. I tell her I'm Alf Santorello's grandson. I'm just out giving Reggie a little exercise, I say, since my nono broke his ankle. She says she's sorry to hear that, but it's nice to meet me—and nice, finally, to learn Reggie's name. "I'm Jenny," she says. But she still doesn't come over.

"Nicky," I say. "Nicky Santorello."

I should just leave well enough alone. But for some reason I can't. I tell this Jenny person I'm only visiting Boston for a short while. I tell her my mom and I are actually from California. (Isn't that where the old guys at the monument told me Old Alf had a daughter?) I tell her we'll be headed back to the beach as soon as Nono's up on his feet. Suddenly I get this really crafty, undercover-type idea, one Dr. Ice would be proud of—if he actually existed. I admit to Jenny that, since I'm not really used to the neighborhood yet, I'm a little turned around. I ask her if she can give me directions back to my grandpa's house.

"Sorry," she says. "I'm new to the neighborhood myself. I've only owned this house a few months."

"Oh," I say. Rats. But at least that explains why she's less friendly with Reggie than, say, Sal or Mrs. Strazzulo.

Jenny tells me it's good to see Reggie's not limping today. I hold up the oily package. That's on account of the bones Mrs. Strazzulo down at the butcher shop saves him, I tell her. Shepherds need the extra calcium. You got to watch those hips with shepherds. Jenny says she'd better get back to her window boxes, it'll be getting dark soon. We say *Nice meeting you* and I give Reggie's leash a little shake. We're off.

The houses start getting run-down again by the time we're on Salem Street, passing by Baldwin Place. By Noyes Place it's definitely transitional. I feel safe enough, though. Who's going to mess with an eighty-pound shepherd?

Reggie comes skidding to a stop in front of the most run-down town house on the block, one that looks a little haunted, if you believe in that sort of thing.

"Now what?" I say. His ears have gone all flat. He's, like, frozen to the spot. I tug on his leash—we've really got to be getting back, it's starting to get dark—but Reggie refuses to budge. I look around. At the next corner there's a sign for Prince Street. So we must have done a big loop. "We gotta go," I say to Reggie. "Mom's probably going mental."

He doesn't budge.

I yank harder on the leash. Finally he moves. But it's not forward. He crosses the street and tiptoes along the sidewalk on the other side. After a half a block, though, he crosses back and carries on like nothing happened. Suddenly he's making a left onto Prince Street and a beeline for supper.

Highly suspicious behavior, if you'd ask me.

About halfway across the bridge, I try to get Reggie to slow down. I'm out of breath, plus there's a really cool view of Old Ironsides, an old-fashioned warship, off to the right. I know for a fact it's the last stop on the Freedom Trail. I've actually stood on its decks with my dad. Supposedly, Old Ironsides is the oldest warship still in use by the U.S. Navy—since the seventeen hundreds. The naval officer who gave Dad and me our tour told us the ship's real name is the USS *Constitution*. Old Ironsides is only the nickname its crew gave it during the War of 1812, because British cannonballs seemed to bounce off it, thanks to the *copper*— not iron—armor Paul Revere had made for its sides.

Dad and I did the Freedom Trail the same day we went to the All-Star Wrestling Extravaganza at Boston Garden, over on the other side of the bridge. One of the best days of my life. One of the few. But that story's still going to have to wait for some other time. Right now we'd better get our butts back to Eden Street before we blow our cover.

TUESDAY NIGHT.
BACK AT THE APARTMENT.

It smells like spaghetti as I'm unlocking the front door. I wonder, for a split second, if I'm in the right place. Yup.

Same old furniture. Same weird-colored carpet, now spotted with a few greenish-brown stains. But Mom isn't slumped in front of the TV as usual. I can hear her in the kitchen chopping up something on the cutting board. Pardon my surprise, but it's been a while since we've had anything around here that wasn't from a takeout box.

So maybe it's going to be a good night.

Back in Littleton, it used to smell like cooking all the time. When I got home from school, I always knew what we were having for supper the second I walked through the door: spaghetti or macaroni and cheese if Mom was making one of my favorites, Thai beef salad or seafood crêpes if she was treating herself, pork chops or roast chicken with all the fixings if she was trying to make Dad—

Well, anyway, the rest of the time.

"We're back," I say, unhooking Reggie's leash. He sniffs the air. You can practically see that big cartoon question mark over his head. I pat him just to let him know everything's OK. I hope.

"Where have you been?" Mom calls from the kitchen. "Dinner's almost ready."

I don't answer. I poke my head in there to see what's up. Reggie cranes his neck around my leg.

"What's that?" she says, pointing her wooden spoon at the greasy package from the butcher shop.

Think quick, Nicky. "Some lady down the street gave me a bag of bones for Reggie," I say.

Mom frowns. "What lady?" she says.

"She's OK," I say. "She's about a thousand years old. She doesn't have anybody to give bones to since her own dog died." Not the total truth, technically speaking, but I'm undercover.

Mom doesn't say anything. I can tell by the too-fast way she's stirring the pot of sauce that she's not convinced.

"They're good for Reggie's hips," I say. "The lady told me she used to have a shepherd herself. That's why she stopped to chat. I haven't even waved hello to anybody else in the neighborhood." That seems to do the trick. Mom stops stirring and smiles. "We're having spaghetti tonight," she says.

Obviously.

"What's the occasion?" I say.

"Do I need a reason to make dinner?" she says.

I don't go there.

"Well, don't just stand there," she says. "Set the table."

"Let me just give Reggie one of these," I say. I open the butcher's paper. Inside are three big bones with little shreds of red meat still clinging to them. I don't even want to guess what part of which animal they're from. "Gross," I say, taking out one.

We both laugh.

Reggie doesn't think they're gross, though. He's licking his chops. Good thing. There's hardly any dog food left for his supper. Again.

"Make him eat that in here on the linoleum," Mom says. "The living room can't really take any more of his decorating."

Let it go, Nicky.

I hand Reggie the bone. He takes it over to his favorite corner by the fridge, lies down, and begins gnawing. His teeth clacking against the bone reminds me of the old guys' bocce balls smacking into each other up at the monument. I don't say this to Mom. No need to go opening *that* can of worms. I just set the table in the other room.

"Isn't this nice?" Mom says when we sit down to eat. She raises her wineglass for a toast. I clink with her—except my glass has fruit punch in it—and we dig in. It is nice. We've laid out the antique tablecloth Mom got from her grandmother. We're using the good china. We've lit candles.

"What's put you in such a good mood?" I say.

"It's our one-month anniversary here," she says, sipping her wine. "It's just time to settle in, that's all. Time to get things, you know, back to normal."

Settling into this dump is NOT getting things back to normal. But I don't say that to her. I'm just letting things go tonight. I twirl a big wad of spaghetti onto my fork and shove it into my mouth.

"So tell me about your day," she says.

I point to my full mouth. She waits. "Not much to tell," I say—when it's clear she expects me to, you know, *talk* with her. "Same old, same old."

"Did you and Mr. Gilmore have a little chat?" she says.

"When did you call him?" I say.

"I was overdue for a teacher-parent conference anyway. So I brought up how unchallenged you were. He said he had a few ideas about how he could fix that. But I insisted he talk the situation over with you directly. Did he?"

Another mark against her in the mental log. Of course that's not how it went. She totally called him as soon as she got to the Ambulance Chasers this morning. And the two of them cooked up this whole independent study thing together. "Yeah," I say.

"Oh good," she says. "I was hoping you guys could work something out man-to-man."

I take another big mouthful of spaghetti.

Man-to-man. She's got this thing, lately, where she's constantly saying stuff like: *I need you to be a little man about it* or *You're the man of the house now.* As if! I won't even be a teenager for, like, another year and three months.

"What's wrong?" she says. "Your face is all red."

I swallow hard. "Nothing."

"So what did you and Mr. Gilmore decide?"

"Book report."

"About what?"

"Can't we just have a normal dinner?" I say.

"That's what I'm trying to do," she says. "You converse at a family dinner. You share the events of your day. You communicate your feelings."

"Well, that approach hasn't exactly worked so hot in the past, has it?" I say.

I swear it slips out before I can bite my tongue.

"What's that supposed to mean?" Mom says.

"Nothing, forget it," I say.

"No, tell me what you meant."

Why isn't she letting this go? I shove more spaghetti into my mouth, but it's getting cold now, and when I try to swallow, it gets stuck in the back of my throat. I take a sip of punch to force it down.

"You're referring to that night with your dad, aren't you?" Mom says, taking a sip of wine. "Good. Let's talk about it, then. Let's finally get everything out in the open. It'll be good for both of us."

I'm never going to drink wine—ever. It makes people say all sorts of stupid things they never should have said and only end up regretting afterward.

"No it won't," I say.

"Yes it will," she says.

Suddenly all I can see is our kitchen back in Littleton. Mom's standing there speechless. There's a gigantic splash of mustard on the wall over her shoulder, shaped like a big, yellow sun.

I try to shove another forkful of spaghetti into my mouth. It won't go down this time. A glob of something gets stuck in my windpipe. I begin to cough.

"Are you OK?" Mom says. "Take a sip of something."

I take another gulp of fruit punch, but this time it doesn't help. I spray red liquid and little brown chunks of meatball all over the tablecloth.

"Stand up, Nicky!" Mom says.

I try, but I still can't catch my breath. There's a pounding in my ears, like the pounding on my old bedroom door after I've locked myself inside, after I've told them both to go away—I don't care if it was all a big misunderstanding.

Maybe it's just the landlord pounding on his ceiling with a broom.

Mom comes around behind me, jams her thumbs into my chest, and squeezes me with her arms. Whatever is stuck pops free.

"Can you breathe now?" she says.

I nod. Her grandmother's tablecloth is ruined, and there's spaghetti chunks all over the carpet.

"Oh Nicky," Mom says in that watery voice that means she's close to tears.

"I'd better get the sponge mop," I say. "This hasn't been a very good week for the security deposit, has it?"

"Oh Nicky!" Mom says again, this time in a whisper.

WEDNESDAY AFTERNOON.
THE SHRINK'S OFFICE, CAMBRIDGE.

D r. Holkke can barely wait until I'm settled into my chair before he starts asking me how things are going this week.

Where do I begin? On the one hand, I got Timmy Burns thinking I'm the class brownie. On the other, I got Rita de la Cruz—thinking my name *is* Brownie—following me around like a dog, making things worse. Then I got a real dog with the name Reggie who refuses to follow me at all, but drags me all over the neighborhood like I'm blind. And then I got a mom who can't see what's plain in front of her face: that things are *not* back to normal living in a crummy one-bedroom apartment in Charlestown.

"Fine," I say.

"Really?" Dr. Holkke says. "Everything's fine? That surprises me. I know how hard settling into a completely new life can be for a kid."

As if! When was the last time he was a kid? He's, like, way over thirty. Plus he's not even an American. Supposedly he's from Sweden, which, according to my social studies book, is one of the Scandinavian countries, along with Norway and Denmark, where the Vikings came from. It was the Vikings, supposedly, and not Columbus who really discovered America.

Dr. Holkke is always reminding me to call him by his first name, which is Håkan. In Sweden, you pronounce the A-on-a-keychain like an O. I always say, *Sure, whatever*, but I don't call him anything.

"You must at least miss your dad," Dr. Holkke says.

"I'm doing OK," I say. And then I just sit there.

After a while, Dr. Holkke clears his throat and asks me what I'm thinking about.

"Nothing much," I say.

"You're not thinking about anything?" he says.

"Not really," I say. But here's what's actually going through my mind: that when you say his name backward—Holkke Håkan—it sounds like the most famous professional wrestler of all time. I don't tell him that, though. I'm sure he has no clue.

"Let's do a role-play," Dr. Holkke says. "Do you know what a role-play is?"

"Like acting?" I say.

"A little," he says. "Only you'll still play the part of you, Nicky, and I'll play the part of someone else. Then we'll think up an interesting situation and act it out."

"Why?" I say.

"To get us talking. The role-play could be about almost anything, really. But how about if we pretend, say, that I'm your dad and that you've just called me up to tell me all about your new life in Boston."

See, what did I tell you? He's obsessed with my dad.

"Why?" I say again.

"Why not?" he says.

My dad knocking on my bedroom door the morning after the mustard thing, asking me to open up and let him in. Him standing there with two suitcases explaining how it was all just a big misunderstanding, how he's moving into a motel for a few days while he works things out with Mom. Me saying, But Fourth of July weekend is coming right up—

what about our trip to Cape Cod? Him saying, We'll just have to see. Meantime he promises to call me every day to check on how I'm doing.

"It's kind of a sore subject with me," I tell Dr. Holkke.

"That's what makes it a good role-play," Dr. Holkke says. "Sometimes it's helpful to act out difficult conversations you cannot have with people in real life."

"I don't see how," I say.

More silence.

"You don't really care for me, do you?" Dr. Holkke says.

I shrug.

"Can I ask you why not?"

"You're always trying to push my buttons," I say.

He chuckles. "That's sort of my job," he says.

"Well, if it were my job, I'd be looking in the want ads," I say.

He chuckles again, but this time I can tell he doesn't think it's so funny.

Then we sit there, just like that, staring at each other, until it's almost time for Mom to take her turn—when I'm sure ol' Holkke Håkan'll get an earful about last night's little dinner party. Dr. Holkke clears his throat. "You know," he says, "some people actually look forward to their visits with me. They find it really helpful to talk about things that are bothering them."

Like your stupid name, for example?

"It's a sort of release for them," he says.

"I'll bear that in mind," I say.

"See you next week," he says.

A LITTLE LATER, WEDNESDAY. DRIVING BACK TO CHARLESTOWN.

Hey, we need to stop by the Supa-Sava," I say to Mom. She hasn't taken the turn lane for the strip mall.

"I'll go tomorrow after work," she says—her first words to me since leaving Dr. Holkke's office.

"But Reggie's out of food," I say. Again.

"He can have leftover spaghetti," she says. "Just like the rest of us."

Truth is, I don't feel like leftover spaghetti myself, not after last night. But I don't push it. I turn on the radio and we listen to the news the rest of the way back to Eden Street. As soon as I step through the door, I grab Reggie's leash and hook it onto his collar.

"Make your bed first," Mom says, pointing at the sleeper sofa. "You're supposed to do it before you leave for school."

"I'll do it the second I get back," I say. "Reggie's been cooped up inside all day."

"Please don't start with me," Mom says with a sigh.

Start what? Reggie's probably bursting for a pee. I don't say anything, though. It was her good lace tablecloth. I just drop Reggie's leash, rip all the bedding off the foldout mattress, and shove it into the linen closet. I stow the mattress, toss the seat cushions back on top, and slide the coffee table into place.

Mom slumps onto the sofa. "There's dog hair all over this," she says, plucking at one of the cushions. "God, there's dog hair all over everything." Her voice is flat and lifeless, like a computer error message.

"No there's not," I say. But there totally is, plain as day.

"What was I thinking?" Mom says. "This apartment is way too small for such a big dog. Plus he's one big fat expense we don't need right now. Plus the landlord will probably evict us as soon as he sees that poor carpet. Maybe I *should* take Reggie back at the end of his trial period."

My stomach flips over. "What trial period?" I say.

"Didn't I tell you?" she says. "The pound gave me a month to decide whether or not it's working out. So far Reggie's been nothing but trouble with a capital *T*. Look at that carpet. Look at my philodendron. And Granny's poor tablecloth! Anyway, there's something not quite right about that dog, something strange I can't put my finger on. Why else would his first master get rid of him?"

"Oh, he's not so bad," I say. "Besides, the tablecloth was my fault."

"He's a lot more work than I expected," Mom says.

As if! She hasn't lifted a finger for Reggie since we got him. I'm the one who feeds him and walks him every day! "I'll vacuum up just as soon as we get back from our walk, OK?" I say.

She sighs and shakes her head.

"I don't mind walking Reggie, honest," I say. I know he's absolutely dancing for a pee right now, but I've got to nip this conversation in the bud.

"Dr. Holkke worries that Reggie may be tying us down too much, preventing us from making new friends," Mom says.

Totally not true, at least not for me. The only reason I know anybody at all in Charlestown is thanks to Reggie: Sal and Floyd and Mickey up at the monument, Mrs. Strazzulo and Jenny in the North End. Too bad I can't tell Mom that.

"Let's just give it to the end of the month, OK?"

She doesn't say anything. She stares at the blank TV screen.

"It was really nice of you to make spaghetti last night," I say.

Her eyes well up with tears. She nods.

I swear to her I'll be right back to vacuum, and then I lead Reggie out the door and down the stoop. I take him over to his favorite hydrant so he can do his business.

Now I've got to step up my investigation. I'm officially on a deadline. I've got a little over three weeks to find out why Old Alf took Reggie to the pound. Before, I was just keeping a mental log of any clues to pass the time. Now I actually need cold, hard evidence to clear his name. I need to prove to Mom that it wasn't Reggie's fault, that there's nothing really wrong with Reggie apart from a slightly rocky start with us. That after breaking his ankle, Old Alf probably just couldn't take care of Reggie.

I sure hope that's all it was. Call it detective's intuition, but I've got this funny feeling the more I dig into the past, the more I'm going to find.

LATER STILL, WEDNESDAY. UP AT THE MONUMENT.

I pretend I just happen to be running into Sal and Floyd and Mickey. But as long as I'm here, I say, I've got a question for them: Have they ever noticed Reggie acting a little strange?

They all give each other this look.

"Oh no," Sal says. "Reggie's never looked better."

"He's not limping, for one," Floyd says.

"Plus that dog really seems to like *you*," Mickey says.

This sets all three of them to chuckling.

"What's that supposed to mean?" I say. "Doesn't Reggie like Grandpa Alf?"

"Ever hear the expression *You can't teach an old dog new tricks*?" Mickey says, winking to the others.

"Sure, everybody has," I say.

"That's enough now, Mickey," Sal says.

"What?" I say.

"Let's just say that expression applied to both Reggie and Old Alf when it came to this guide-dog business," Sal says.

"Your granddad was a lot more used to a cane," Floyd says.

Mickey starts chuckling again. I ask him to let me in on the joke, but Sal says Mickey's already said quite enough for one day. Mickey pipes up that they still need a fourth for their afternoon bocce. Did my granddad ever tell me why he doesn't come around to the monument anymore?

Think quick, Nicky.

I tell them they may as well have the whole story—since we're all friends now. The reason they haven't seen Old Alf, I say, is because he's been laid up with a broken ankle. He took a fall right outside his house in the North End. And though I don't have all the details, I say—you know how grown-ups are around kids—my mom and I took the first flight out from California to look after him while he was in a cast.

"Well, why didn't you say so in the first place?" Mickey says.

"Oh, we understand," Sal says, winking. "You did the right thing by not broadcasting your granddad's private business all over Charlestown."

"Is Old Alf going to be OK?" Floyd says. "It ain't so easy to heal your bones when you're his age."

"I'll keep you posted," I say. "Meantime, Grandpa Alf gave me the responsibility of making sure Reggie stays in tip-top condition." I tell them I've got to hoof it over to the North End before Mrs. Strazzulo closes up for the day. I explain how she's saving all the spare bones for Reggie's hip. They all nod their heads and give Reggie's right haunch a couple of extra strokes before we take off for the Charlestown Bridge.

Mrs. Strazzulo is just starting to roll up the striped awning outside her butcher shop when we finally get to Hanover Street. I ask her if she has any bones. She nods and hands me the metal crank. She warns me not to turn it too tight at the end or the awning will get stuck. She goes inside while Reggie and I crank up the rest of the awning. People smile at me as they're passing by, and I smile back—pretending for a minute that I work for Mrs. Strazzulo after school and this is all part of the job. She comes back with the same kind of greasy package as before.

"Did you ask your nono if he wants any meat from Strazzulo's?"

I hesitate a second. Then, before I quite know why, I blurt, "Nono said he'll take the cutlets."

"How many?" she says.

"Four," I say. "One for each of us—Nono, Mom, me, and Reggie—if you can put that on account for him, that is." What the heck am I saying?

Just be cool, Nicky. You're undercover.

"Don't just stand there," she says. "You'll let the flies in."

Reggie and I follow her into the shop.

"Your nono must have buried the hatchet with Reggie," she says. "To treat him to his own piece of veal."

"What hatchet?" I say.

"None of my business," she says, weighing up four veal cutlets, while I try not to freak out about how much they cost a pound. "But I'm surprised he decided to hang on to that dog."

"Why do you say that?"

"Way I hear it, the accident was all Reggie's fault," she says. She takes the package of bones from me and puts it in a bag with the cutlets. "Mailman told me it was Reggie's job to make sure your nono didn't step into the street if there was any danger. But he did, and one of those crazy bike messengers sideswiped him, right in front of his house, without even looking back. Your nono lay there with a broken ankle for I don't know how long before the mailman finally came across him on his daily rounds. According to the mailman, Reggie was just sitting there panting like nothing was wrong. He was sure your nono was going to get rid of Reggie after that. In fact he was really surprised when I told him Mr. Santorello's grandson was still coming by here with the dog to pick up bones."

"Well, thanks for the meat," I say. Because I can't think of anything else.

"None of my business," Mrs. Strazzulo says. "Now get out of here. I got rabbits to skin."

I give Reggie a good, long stare as soon as we're safely on Parmenter Street. Sorry, but he just doesn't look like the type who would deliberately harm his master. Plus he totally protected me against those Townies on Monday. More likely, Old Alf just didn't understand the right guide-dog commands. Floyd said himself Old Alf was better with a cane.

Jenny is out on her front steps reading the *Boston Globe* when Reggie and I get to Bartlett Place. I wave hello. She waves back. "How's your grandfather doing?" she calls over. She's still keeping her distance.

"About the same," I say. "Can I ask you a question?"

"Of course," she says.

"How come you don't pet Reggie? Did he ever do something to make you afraid of him?"

"Honestly?" she says. She gets up and wanders over to the iron fence that runs along the sidewalk where we're standing. "Your granddad got kind of upset with me the first time I tried. He told me Reggie's not a pet so I shouldn't make a fuss over him. I guess you're not supposed to pet guide dogs when they're on duty. Anyway, I apologized and I stopped."

Very interesting. I add this to my mental log.

"Well, Reggie's not on duty now," I say.

Jenny smiles. She stoops down and gives Reggie a good, long scratch behind his ears. I tell her I'd better get going, since I've got dinner. I hold up the bag with the cutlets. She laughs. We both say *See you soon.* Then Reggie and I shove off. Halfway across the Charlestown Bridge, I open the bag and feed Reggie all the cutlets. It's only fair since there isn't any canned food for him tonight.

Boston Garden is all lit up. While Reggie wolfs down his veal, I think of that other story for another time. We made a whole day of it, Dad and me. We went into the city on the commuter train, we walked the Freedom Trail, and we saw nearly every sight there was to see. We went out for pizza afterward, and then we went to Boston Garden for the All-Star Wrestling Extravaganza. Our seats were just three rows back from the ring. We watched the most famous wrestlers in the world slam each other around, right in front of us. And even though we could both see it was kind of fake—most of the time they were only pretending to hit each other—we both shouted and clapped like crazy, cheering all the good guys to victory and booing all the villains to defeat.

Reggie tugs on his leash. I need to figure out whether he was a bad guide dog like Mrs. Strazzulo says, or whether Old Alf and Reggie just couldn't get it together as a team, like Mickey says. The only way I'll know for sure is to learn as much as possible about the job of a seeing-eye. So it's a good thing I start my independent study tomorrow afternoon. I can hardly wait to hit the books in the library.

First, though, I've got all this vacuuming to do before leftover spaghetti.

THURSDAY. BEGINNING OF ENGLISH PERIOD.

Mr. Gilmore hands me a pass for the library just like he said. He tells me to take my coat and stuff with me. I don't have to come back to homeroom after the final bell.

"Wait a second," Timmy Burns says. "Why does Brownie get to skip class?"

"His name's Nicky, not Brownie," Gilmore says. "And the matter doesn't concern you, Timmy."

"*My* name's Tim, not Timmy."

Everybody laughs at this.

"As a matter of fact, I want all of you to take out your English books," Gilmore says, "and turn to page one fifty-six."

I gather up my stuff. Everybody but Timmy turns to page one fifty-six. He just sits there with his arms crossed.

"Is there a problem?" Gilmore says to him.

"It's not fair," Timmy says. "I'm going to tell my dad about this. He's on the PTA."

"While you're at it, be sure to remind him what you got on your last Robert Frost quiz," Gilmore says.

Everybody laughs. Oh great.

I head for the door. Gilmore winks at me all buddy-buddy and says, "See you tomorrow, Nicky."

I know he thinks he's helping me out, but he isn't. Now I'm hosed with Timmy Burns and his posse for, like, the rest of my life.

I show my pass to the librarian, Ms. Klee. She's this really pretty black woman who either wears her hair in cornrows or wraps it all up in a high, colorful turban, even though she's American, not African. Well, she's probably *originally* from Africa, like I'm originally from Ireland. Nobody's originally from America, not even the Native

Americans. Supposedly, they crossed over here from Asia a gazillion years ago on that tail of Alaska when it was still hooked up to Russia. Anyway, Ms. Klee tells me she's been expecting me. She says she's glad for the company, and it's true, the library *is* pretty empty. She takes me over to a carrel by the window.

"This can be your desk," she says. "Just make yourself at home. You can even leave books or whatever you're working on right here. I won't let anyone mess with your stuff."

I put my coat on the back of the chair. I can tell immediately that Ms. Klee and I are going to get along.

"You're doing your project on dogs, right?" she says.

"Not just dogs," I say. "Seeing-eye dogs."

"Cool," she says. "Let's go look in the card catalog."

Before you know it, she's got me set up in my carrel with a fresh pad of paper and a couple of books. She says that ought to get me rolling. Meanwhile she'll have a look online. Maybe there are a couple of Web sites on the subject.

I open up one of the books and begin reading.

Here's what I learn, just from the first ten pages.

They're not called seeing-eye dogs anymore. Blind people prefer "guide dog" or "assistance dog" because, for them, getting around isn't about, you know, *seeing*. Three breeds of canine are usually trained to be guide dogs. German shepherds are the most popular by far. But golden retrievers and Labs are also trained to guide. These particular breeds are chosen because of their intelligence, willingness, and temperament.

I mark my page by putting my finger in the book. I stare out the window and watch people passing by on the street below. People I don't know. People I'll never meet, hurrying to unknown places. I touch the side of the carrel. Mine— mine only. Suddenly I don't care if I'm hosed with Timmy Burns. It's so quiet here. You can really think in a library. You can really get a lot of thinking done.

THURSDAY, FINAL BELL. THE LIBRARY.

I pack my knapsack and straighten up my new carrel. I say good-bye to Ms. Klee and head for the main lobby. All in all, a very productive afternoon of digging for clues. Turns out guide dogs start their training when they're just eight-week-old puppies. They're in school for about a year and a half. Someone called a puppy raiser teaches them all the basics, like obedience and manners. (That could be anybody, by the way: you and me—convicts, even—anyone who likes dogs.) When the dogs are old enough, though, a professional trainer at an actual guide-dog school takes over to teach them how to judge distances and avoid obstacles. This can take up to six months. Finally the blind master works with both the trainer and the dog for another month to learn all the commands. The whole process can cost thirty thousand dollars a dog. Luckily the blind master never has to pay a penny. Training schools usually get companies, or sometimes movie stars, to sponsor dogs.

Oh great.

Timmy Burns is waiting for me outside the school's front gates. Not just him, but Johnny Hedges and Chris McDuff and some other Townie kid who isn't even in our homeroom. I pretend I don't notice them. I fish around in my knapsack as if I'm looking for my keys. I try to walk past. Yeah, right. They form a circle around me, like the Heat around Dr. Ice in nearly every episode.

"What?" I say. I stick my hands in my pockets, just in case they start shaking. According to Marky, you're totally done for the second a bully sees you're afraid. Funny. I just learned in the library that dogs can literally smell emotions like fear and anger and danger. Their keen sense of smell picks up these little molecules of scent you give off called pheromones. That's why dogs make such good guides—they can anticipate trouble for their masters. They can smell it.

Boy do I wish Reggie was here right now, to let off one of his Townie warning growls.

"Well, if it isn't Brownie the class genius," Timmy Burns says.

"The name's Nicky," I say. "And I'm not that smart."

"So how come you're Gilmore's crack monitor then?"

Bullies will never stop messing with you if they think you're afraid, Marky told me. And he knows. He's had to deal with the likes of Timmy Burns every time his dad moved army bases. Marky's advice: *The best defense is offense.*

I decide to go for it.

"I can't help it if this school is full of idiots," I say.

That surprises Timmy. Good.

"Looks like we've got ourselves a wise guy," he says to his posse. But it's a pretty lame comeback, and he knows it.

Never act scared at any cost. Marky's dad taught him that. His dad looks really mean—he has a crew cut and is super-fit from doing hundreds of push-ups a day—but he's actually pretty nice. He just doesn't want his troops to know that, because he needs to keep the upper hand.

"Look," I say, "if you're going to beat me up, let's just get it over with. You guys can obviously take me. It's, like, four against one."

"I've got your back, Brownie!"

Rita leaps out from behind a parked VW. I watch in horror as she comes flying up over the back bumper and lands between me and the Townie posse in what looks like a karate stance.

"Have no fear, Rita's here," she says.

"My name isn't Brownie," I say.

"If it isn't your girlfriend, Ladybug," Timmy says.

"She isn't my girlfriend," I say.

"Put up or shut up, *pendejo!*" Rita says to Timmy.

"I don't fight girls," Timmy says. "Townie rules."

"But four against one is OK, I guess, as long as it's a

guy?" Rita says. "Your Townie rules suck, carrot top!" She does a roundhouse kick that knocks the Red Sox cap off Timmy's head.

Timmy's posse bursts into laughter.

Timmy bends down. He picks up his cap. He jams it back onto his head. His face is as red as the *B* on the front.

"I can definitely take you myself," he says to me. "And I'll prove it at lunchtime tomorrow, right here on this playground, right in front of the whole school." He starts to walk away. "Come on, guys," he says. "It stinks like brown-nose around here."

I stare after them.

Rita turns to me, smiling.

"That was SO not helpful," I say. I stride off in the direction of Eden Street.

Rita falls into step beside me. "So what *is* your real name, if it isn't Brownie?"

I whirl on her, furious. "Just leave me alone, OK?"

"I was thinking more along the lines of a quick game of Ultimate," she says. She starts pulling a Frisbee out of her knapsack.

"You're that really weird girl in every school," I say. "The one everybody hates, who ambushes all the new kids and tries to make friends with them before they figure out nobody normal will actually talk to you."

Rita stops following. She shoves the Frisbee back in her bag. "Wow, that was really harsh," she says.

"I don't want to play Frisbee with you," I say. "I don't want to eat lunch with you. I don't want to hang out with you. I wish you would just go away and stop bothering me."

Rita throws up her hands and backs off. "*Lo siento mucho*," she says. "I just thought you were, you know, *different* from the other boneheads around here." She strides off in the opposite direction, but then turns back. "P.S.," she says. "That really weird girl you're talking about? Lulu McFadden. She eats dirt."

I watch Rita disappear around the corner.

Thing is, I don't *want* to be different. I can't even tell you how tired I am of sticking out, of feeling weird—of people pointing when they think I'm not looking and whispering behind my back: *See him? That's the kid who . . .*

It's a dog-eat-dog world out there. Belonging to the right group is totally a matter of survival.

LATER THURSDAY. UP AT THE MONUMENT.

*S*al hands me a get-well-soon card. He says it's for Old Alf from the three of them—him and Floyd and Mickey. I tuck it into my back pocket and promise to give it to Grandpa as soon as I get home. Floyd asks for an update on how things are going. I say whatever comes to mind: what we had for dinner last night (veal cutlets), who won at Monopoly (him, even though I could have pulled a few fast ones as banker), what TV shows we watched (*Who Wants to Be a Genius?* and *Cops on the Beat*), and what I read to him before bed (some of a book on how guide dogs are trained). The old guys hang on every word. I guess they don't have nearly as much fun with their own grandkids.

"So what's the story with his broken ankle?" Sal says.

"It's definitely healing," I say. "But the doctor still doesn't know how long it will be before he's back on his feet."

"Hard to believe he fell right outside his own house," Floyd says. "He's lived there his whole life."

"Yeah," Mickey says. "Something fishy about that."

I look down at Reggie, who's lying at my feet. Do I tell them what Mrs. Strazzulo said?

"Muggers," I say. "On bikes with ski masks. Supposedly the next-door neighbor witnessed the whole thing. Grandpa was coming out of his house with Reggie when a gang of roving Townies on BMX bikes came swooping around the corner and sideswiped him for his wallet. Reggie tried to chase after them, but they were way too fast. So Reggie set off to find help. He brought the mailman back from Hanover Street, who, when he saw Grandpa lying on the sidewalk, called 911 from his cell phone."

They all give the dog pats on the back and scratches behind the ears.

"Golly," Sal says. "Reggie did that?"

"Surprised we haven't seen it in the papers," Floyd says.

"How come you didn't tell us any of this before now?" Mickey says.

"You know how Grandpa is about broadcasting family business," I say.

I know I'm going to get caught, just in case you're wondering. It's only a matter of time before Alf Santorello comes strolling into Monument Square with his new guide dog. The jig will totally be up then. Then there'll be hell to pay. Meantime I can't seem to stop myself from making up these stories. It's not just about being undercover anymore. It's more like that feeling you get of needing to eat an entire bag of corn chips without stopping, even though you've already had enough after the first couple of handfuls and your mouth hurts from all the salt.

"Forward!" I say, before I make things any worse. Reggie heads for Monument Ave. He pretty much does exactly what I say, now that I've learned some of the basic guide-dog commands doing my independent study in the library. When you want your dog to go straight ahead, for instance, you just say *Forward!* and not *Come on, boy!* or *Let's go!* Turns out, I was already using some of the commands and didn't even know it. Reggie always stopped dead in his tracks whenever I said *Stop!* He turned right if I said *Right!* and left if I said *Left!* Well, most of the time. Anyway, I never actually needed to yank on his leash. I just needed to use the right language. Guide dogs can learn foreign languages, too, no problem, if they're in training for a master who lives in Italy, say, or Sweden. The blind master is always the one who's in control when he knows what to say. The guide dog never makes a decision about where to go, just how to get there.

Just before we walk into the butcher shop, I spy a mailman through the front window, handing Mrs. Strazzulo a bundle of letters over the counter. Reggie still wants to go in, of course. But I make him stop and turn back up Hanover Street. When we get to the corner of Prince, I make him take a right. I'm hoping we can sneak down the next street over and circle around to Parmenter without getting noticed. Frankly, I have no desire to meet Mrs. Strazzulo's mailman at the moment.

We end up at a place called North Square after about a block. Suddenly we're standing in front of this really old wooden building. I know where I am, even before I read the bronze plaque telling me it's Paul Revere's House. I was here a couple of years ago, when Dad and I were doing the Freedom Trail. Supposedly Paul Revere, who was a famous silversmith, looked up from making a teapot one night and saw there were two lamps burning in the steeple of the Old North Church, which was the secret signal that the redcoats were planning to invade by sea. So he climbed on his trusty steed and rode across the city, waking up all the neighbors by screaming, *The British are coming! The British are coming!* and they believed him, even though it was kind of a crazy thing to do.

I point out the red-brick line laid into the sidewalk to Reggie. "That's the actual Freedom Trail," I say. "It goes all over Boston connecting the dots between one historic sight, like this place, and the next. If I remember right, the next stop is the Old North Church. Then it eventually goes across the Charlestown Bridge to Old Ironsides. We ought to follow it sometime, just as soon as we wrap up this case." He cocks his head, like he's trying to understand why we would ever do such a thing.

We take North Street out of the square and come to Richmond Street, where we take a right. We practically tiptoe across Hanover below the butcher shop, and suddenly we're on Parmenter—back in familiar territory. Jenny's out in front of her town house, as usual. She's touching up the iron fence along the sidewalk with black paint. This time she reaches down and pets Reggie without even asking. She asks me if I want to grab a paintbrush and help her for a few minutes. I sort of do, actually, but don't want to risk being MIA when Mom gets home from the Ambulance Chasers. I tell her another time. Good, she says. Her little yard isn't very big, but it could use all the help it can get. She's right. It's not much bigger than our apartment's bathroom, but it's totally overgrown with bushes. I tell her I'm no stranger to gardening, since my mom had this really big one back home in . . . um . . . California.

Maybe I won't get caught. Maybe Alf Santorello just

moved away after the accident and didn't feel like telling the whole world about it—like me and Mom. Maybe he went to live with his daughter in California. Maybe that's why Reggie ended up at the pound, because his daughter is super-allergic to dogs or something, and she couldn't have him in the house.

Reggie and I head over the bridge after our usual do-si-do around the spooky house in Noyes Place. I stop. I take the get-well-soon card out of my back pocket. I toss it into the nearest trash can.

Maybe, just maybe, Mom will come to her senses and make up with Dad before the paperwork goes through at the Ambulance Chasers. Maybe we'll get our security deposit back from the landlord here in Charlestown and Dad'll give up his new apartment in Littleton and we'll all move back to our old house and things really will be back to normal by the time the old guys and Mrs. Strazzulo and Jenny put two and two together.

Yeah, right. And maybe Reggie will suddenly learn how to fly.

FRIDAY, LUNCH RECESS.

Mr. Gilmore dismisses us from social studies, and everyone heads for their lockers—except me. I hang back at my desk. I glance around for Timmy Burns. I don't see him, but Johnny Hedges and Chris McDuff both punch my arm as they pass, whispering they'll be waiting for me right outside—it's showtime.

As if.

I take my note up to Mr. Gilmore's desk. "Dentist appointment," I say. "I forgot to show it to you in homeroom, on account of I was a little late."

He looks it over.

"You sure your mom typed this?" he says.

"She's a secretary," I say. "At a law firm."

"She misspelled *excuse*," he says.

"They keep her pretty busy."

He hands me back the note.

"How's your independent study coming?" he says.

"Fine," I say.

"Ms. Klee says you're a hard worker."

I shrug.

"How's everything else going?" he says.

"Fine," I say. What does he mean, everything else? "My mom's probably waiting for me out front," I say.

"Tell her I said hi."

Okeydokey.

I sneak out of the school by the side exit to avoid the Townies on the playground. I'm hoping if Timmy Burns doesn't get to beat me up at lunch recess today, he'll get wrapped up in kickball or picking on some other new kid. So far so good this morning. Apart from the occasional spitball on the back of the neck, I've managed to avoid any direct contact with him during homeroom, math, science, and social studies. Anyway, there wasn't much he could do to me with Gilmore standing right there. I'll be MIA all lunch recess, and afternoons are easy. I take Spanish with Señorita Alvarez, while Timmy takes French with Mademoiselle Colbert. He takes art and I take music. And now I go to the library instead of English.

Plan B for lunch recess: Chase up a few clues in the whole Alf Santorello case.

I sneak down to Medford Street, then hail the first free cab. I tell the driver to take me over to the Back Bay. I should have plenty of money. Before Mom left for work this morning, I told her I needed twenty dollars for an upcoming field trip to the Museum of Science. At first she had a cow— Twenty dollars? What for? Don't school groups get into museums for free?—so I had to make up some story about how there was a special buffet lunch of space food at the IMAX theater. Luckily she was running late, so she just handed over the money with a big sigh.

The cab lets me off in front of the dog pound in the South End. Well, they don't call it a pound anymore. They call it a rescue shelter. (I looked up the address in the phone book last night. I also looked up Alf Santorello's phone number—just in case you think I'm a total idiot. There weren't any A. Santorellos listed, but that doesn't rule out the possibility he's got an unlisted number.) Not that you would ever need to know the actual street number of the pound, by the way, to guess which building it is. You'd have to be totally deaf not to hear all that barking. Plus you can smell the place a half a block away. It's even worse inside—dog pee and pine cleaner do not mix, let me tell you—and it's hard not to make a face as I mosey all casual-like over to the receptionist at the front desk. "We just got a dog from here," I tell her, "a big shepherd named Reggie."

"The ex-guide dog?"

"That's him," I say. "I was in the neighborhood and was wondering if you could give me the address and phone number of his former blind master."

"Sorry," she says. "I can't."

"I already know his name," I say. "It's Alf Santorello. He's an old Italian guy from the North End. I need to ask him a few dog-related questions."

"I really can't," she says. "I don't know anything about Reggie's life as a guide dog. The family who brought him here said they adopted him from some agency for the blind after he was already retired."

Rats! A dead end. "Oh," I say. "You don't know which agency, do you?"

The receptionist shakes her head. "I think they said it was the place where Reggie got trained. His new family only had him for a few weeks," she says. "And then the father got an unexpected transfer for work. They couldn't take Reggie with them because it was overseas. It was all very last-minute and they were really sad about bringing him here to the shelter."

"Oh," I say again. But it's not a total dead end. I've learned something new: Old Alf didn't lug Reggie off to the pound. He took Reggie back to the local guide-dog school where he was trained. That should be pretty easy to find. I mean, how many could there be in Boston? "That's OK," I say, trying to play it cool. Because suddenly I feel like a *real* detective. "I was just passing by."

"How's Reggie working out?" she says. "He's such a sweetheart."

"Everything's great," I say.

"Oh good," she says. "We love it when matches work out."

"We definitely won't need to be returning him before the end of his trial period," I say for good measure. Not if I can help it, anyway.

I hail another cab once I'm back on the street. I tell the driver the address of my school in Charlestown. My stomach starts to growl as soon as we pass the public library. It's only then that I remember I forgot to sneak my lunch bag out of my locker.

FRIDAY, SPANISH PERIOD—WELL, SUPPOSEDLY. SCHOOL HALLWAY.

I tiptoe over to my locker to grab my lunch and wolf my sandwich before turning up late to Señorita Alvarez's class. Someone has drawn a big nose in brown marker across the front of the locker, then circled it in red marker and put a red slash through it.

I sigh. I open the door. I grab my sandwich out of the bag and take a big bite.

"Young man! What are you doing out here?"

Oh great. The school secretary.

"I was at the dentist," I say. But I don't even sound like I'm speaking English because my mouth is full of PB and J and my tongue is sticking to the roof.

"Do you have a note?" the secretary says.

I reach into my pocket for my fake excuse. When I try to hand it to her, she's staring straight at the marker graffiti on my locker.

"Did you do that?" she says, pointing.

I shake my head.

"Well, who did?" she says.

"Hi, Mrs. Johnston."

We both look around. It's Rita, coming down the hallway, saying good-bye to someone on her pink cell phone.

"Hi, Rita," the secretary says. "The baby sick again?"

Rita nods. "Mom needs me to get back to the house and babysit Julio so she can take the niño to the doctor. I've cleared it all with Mrs. McClafferty. She gave me a bunch of homework to do."

"I hope the doctor figures out what's wrong," Mrs. Johnston says.

"Me too," Rita says, staring at me.

That causes Mrs. Johnston to remember she was chewing me out about the graffiti on my locker. "Vandalizing school property is a serious offense," she says. "It could mean immediate suspension. What do you have to say for yourself?"

"I didn't do it," I say.

"Come with me," she says. "You can explain that to the principal."

"But I'm late for Spanish," I say.

She grabs me by my arm.

"He didn't do it," Rita says.

"This matter doesn't concern you, Rita," she says, dragging me about a foot.

"But he didn't, Mrs. Johnston," Rita says. "That's been there ever since I can remember. Haven't you ever noticed it before?"

"No," Mrs. Johnston says, unsure. "Do you know this student, Rita?"

Rita gives me the up-and-down.

I feel myself going red.

"No," she says. "I've never spoken to him before in my life. He must be new."

She walks off down the hallway, dialing a number on her phone.

"Get to Spanish class," Mrs. Johnston says to me.

▬▬▬

FRIDAY, ENGLISH PERIOD.
SCHOOL LIBRARY.

Finally I'm in my carrel and reading up on guide-dog training schools. I didn't catch much of the rest of Spanish. And now I've got a little bit of a headache, thanks to Mrs. Atkins's music class—twenty-five kids pounding out "Oh, Where Have You Been, Billy Boy, Billy Boy?" on the xylophone for an hour.

Turns out only sixty percent of the dogs make it through school. The rest flunk out and need to get placed into ordinary homes. I guess that's why every school seems to have an adoption agency. Plus most of these agencies find homes for any of the dogs who do graduate from their school but don't work out on the job. That must be the category Reggie is in.

I ask Ms. Klee if I can go online to look up the phone number of the nearest guide-dog training school, so I can interview someone for my project. She has no problem with that. Nor does she have any problem when I hand her the fake dentist appointment note and ask to be excused twenty minutes early. She just smiles and says, "TGIF." That means Thank God it's Friday. But I don't actually see what's so great about the weekends—not now anyway.

In my old neighborhood, weekends were great. I got to play all day Saturday with Marky. We were building a tree fort with his dad just before I moved. His dad got every weekend off from the base. He spent most of the time hanging out with Marky and his brothers and me. We had some fun times together. We all used to camp out in the backyard. I mean camp out *for real*. Marky's dad had an official army tent and mess kits and everything. We even cooked our own food on a hibachi. That's when Marky's mom would usually call up my mom for a girls' night out.

My own dad works a lot on the weekends.

I duck out of the library, dash through the empty corridors, and cut across the playground ages before the final bell—when Timmy Burns will be hunting me down.

Wouldn't it be cool if Dad called Mom at work today, asking if I could come out to Littleton this weekend to help him set up his new apartment. Wouldn't it be great if Mom were in a good enough mood to say, *Sure, I don't see why not—except Nicky has a dog now*. Wouldn't it be even greater if Dad said, *No problem, the more the merrier*. Then Reggie and I would be spending Saturday doing something fun, instead of laundry at the strip mall and groceries at the Supa-Sava. Dad and I always had fun when it was just him and me—like that day we did the Freedom Trail followed by the All-Star Wrestling Extravaganza at Boston Garden. Well, maybe not *always* fun, but most times.

I hoof it back to Eden Street, hook Reggie to his leash, and take him for a walk around the block. I apologize to him for cutting our rounds short today, but I've got an important call to make before Mom gets home.

The operator at the training school asks me how she can direct my call. I tell her I'd like to speak with the person in charge of placing retired guide dogs in people's homes. She asks me to hold while she transfers me to their adoption department. Suddenly I'm listening to boring classical music, like the kind I get stuck hearing in rush-hour traffic with Mom. While I wait, I see if there's anything to eat in the fridge. It seems like forever before another lady finally comes on the line. I ask her if she ever placed a retired shepherd named Reggie in my neighborhood. She wants to know who's calling, please. I tell her I'm Reggie's new master.

"Mrs. Pendleton?" she says. "I didn't recognize your voice."

I try not to get annoyed. "The Pendletons had to move away suddenly," I say. "We got Reggie from the pound."

"Oh, I see," she says. "How may I help you, Mrs.—?"

"Nicholas," I say, going with the flow. I can't *wait* for the day my voice starts to change. "I'm trying to locate Mr. Santorello, Reggie's former blind master," I say. "I'd like to ask him a few questions about Reggie."

"I'm afraid I am unable to discuss the personal information of any of our clients," she says. "We adhere to a strict privacy policy here."

"Oh, it's OK," I say. "Alf Santorello and I go to the same butcher shop in the North End."

"Perhaps I can try fielding your questions?" she says.

Rats! She's definitely not going to leak Old Alf's current whereabouts. But I may as well fish for more info about Reggie, since I've got her on the line and she's pretty much admitted he came through her agency. "Well, for one thing," I say, "I'm curious to know why Reggie got retired."

There's a long pause. I'm pretty sure I'm using the right lingo. According to my research, "retired" is the word all the training schools use when a guide dog gets fired on the job. There are all sorts reasons for early retirement: Dogs develop a medical disability, they're not smart enough to begin with, they don't like to follow their masters' orders once they're trained, or they lose their tempers. They're called career-change dogs, then. But really they just get busted down to the status of regular dog and stuck with a normal family like mine. Well, one that can see, anyway.

"If you're having a problem with Reggie," the lady finally says, "we'd be more than happy to take him back, Mrs. Nicholas. We have quite a waiting list. In fact, the Pendletons waited over a year before Reggie became available. Which is why I'm really surprised to hear they didn't contact us—"

"No, there's no problem," I say. "Except for his hips. But I'm giving him bones from the butcher shop."

"You need to watch the right one in particular," she says.

"Is that why Reggie was retired—on a medical disability?"

"I suppose you have the right to know the particulars of

Reggie's reassignment," the lady says. "Even if you didn't acquire him through us. But since the matter is a delicate one, I would really prefer to discuss it in person. Perhaps you could make an appointment—"

I hear Mom's key in the lock. I hang up. I grab my pitcher of fruit punch from the fridge, trying to act natural.

"Were you just on the phone?" she says, as soon as she gets to the kitchen.

"Nope," I say.

"I swear I heard you talking with someone in here," she says.

"I was just telling Reggie what a good boy he is. Wasn't I, fella?"

He looks up from his bone with one of those *What did I do?* expressions.

"Oh," she says. "God, what a diabolical day I've had!"

"TGIF," I say. "Hey, speaking of phone calls, Dad didn't call you at work to set up something for this weekend, did he?"

"What do *you* think?" she says. She hauls her jug of vino out of the fridge. She hesitates before reaching for a wineglass on the drying rack. "He did e-mail me, though. He wrote that he forgot he had some big sales conference in Las Vegas this weekend. He promised to set something up as soon as he's back."

"Oh," I say. I take a gulp of punch.

There's so much on the tip of my tongue. But I don't

go there. What would be the point? I just put another check mark next to Mom in my mental log.

SATURDAY MORNING. ON THE WAY TO THE STRIP MALL—OR ARE WE?

Hey, wait a minute," I say. "You missed the turnoff to the Supa-Sava." We're headed for the community college, as though we're on our way to Dr. Holkke's in Cambridge.

"I have to swing by the office," she says. "I left my paycheck on my desk. I need to cash it before we can buy the groceries. Plus we need quarters for the machines."

We used to have a whole laundry room in our old house back in Littleton.

I turn on the radio. She's left it on the rock station again. This particular hair band is supposedly in some sort of purple haze.

"Hey, how's that project at school going?" Mom says, turning the volume way down. "It's about dogs, right?"

Not just dogs. Guide dogs. "Fine," I say.

"Well, tell me about it," she says.

"How long are we going to be at your office?" I say.

"Oh, not too long," she says.

I don't like the sound of that. I turn the radio back up.

A few minutes later we're crossing the Charles River at the Salt and Pepper Bridge. (That's not its real name, by the way. It's the Longfellow Bridge. Supposedly, it got that nickname because the little towers holding it up are shaped like salt and pepper shakers.) I like the view from the top. You can see the whole city: Beacon Hill, where the capitol dome is; the skyscrapers of Downtown; the skyscrapers of Back Bay, sailboats darting up and down the river. It's a bright, sunny day with lots of puffy white clouds. It looks just like a postcard of Boston, instead of the real thing. Chugging up the other side of the Charles, I spy one of those duck boats that go on water as well as land. Man, am I dying to take one of those tours!

On our left, a Red Line train pulls alongside our car. The T crosses over the Charles at the Salt and Pepper Bridge. I pretend we're racing it. The best part is, I know we'll beat all those grown-ups inside reading newspapers, because the train has to slow down for its next stop at the end of the bridge.

Sometimes it's nice to know you're guaranteed to win at something.

We make a right turn onto Charles Street and pull into an alley, which is also the Ambulance Chasers' parking lot. Mom takes the space next to a black Benz convertible. So Chaser Junior must be inside.

"I'll wait out here," I say.

"Come in and say hello," Mom says.

"Do I have to?" I say.

"It's not going to kill you to be polite," she says. She waits for me to open my door. I don't. She sighs. "Whatever," she says, going all stony-faced. "Do whatever you want." She opens her door and gets out, leaving the keys in the ignition.

I turn up the radio. Way up. I blast some song about a free bird for a couple of seconds, then I get out too.

As if I really have any choice.

Chaser Junior is chatting with Mom at her desk. He's wearing one of those tracksuit getups that make the *sh* sound when you walk. Usually he wears a shirt and tie to work. Sometimes the tie doesn't quite reach over his belly.

"How you been, Sport?" Chaser Junior says. He calls me sport, which I hate, and ruffles my hair, which I also hate. "I was just telling your mom this is the last place I'd expect to find the two of you on her day off."

"We're only here to pick up her paycheck," I say. "Then we got stuff to do."

Chaser Junior laughs. "Terrific day out there. I was just saying to your mom it's a crime to be wasting it on errands."

Mom tells Chaser Junior he's right, we really ought to be taking advantage of the beautiful fall weather somehow—does he have any suggestions? Chaser Junior winks and says, as a matter of fact, he was just on his way out to pick up his own boys and take them over by the river to the Esplanade. They've made a really nice park for kids over there, he says, with a skateboard ramp and community boating and kite flying—the works. He says lots of single dads take their kids on weekends to throw a ball around, eat a couple of hot dogs, have a few laughs.

He should know, I guess. He's going on something like his fourth wife.

"So how about it?" he says suddenly. To me.

"How about what?" I say.

"You want to come along? I bet we could convince your mom to let you out of doing those errands. I got two nice boys, just about your age."

"No thanks," I say.

"Oh, I don't mind," Mom says.

"We could all go bowling afterward," Chaser Junior says. "Grab a pizza and a pitcher of root beer at the alley for lunch."

"I'll be out in the car," I say, heading for the door.

Because I am so totally out of there.

I turn the radio back on. It's a song about an evil woman. I try to find a decent station, one without hair bands or classical music or people talking about how lousy the Red Sox are. I can't. So I start switching the dial every time there's a commercial, which is a lot. Finally Mom comes out of the office. I can tell by the look on her face I'm in the doghouse. I turn the radio off.

"That was so rude!" she says, slamming the car door. "He was only being nice."

"He was not. He was being totally sketchy," I say.

"Well, you hurt his feelings," she says.

"What do you care?" I say. "You call him names behind his back."

"Oh, he's not so bad," she says.

YOU CAN'T TEACH AN OLD DOG NEW TRICKS

"Fine," I say. "You go fly a kite with him in the park."

She starts the engine and throws the stick shift into reverse. "I can't win!" she says. "I just thought it might be nice for you to be around a few guys for a change."

"Well, then let Dad have me for the weekend," I say.

"What's that supposed to mean?"

"Doesn't it strike you as funny that there's always some last-minute reason why my weekends with him don't work out?" I say.

"That's not because of *me*," she says. "I told you, he e-mailed me at work to say he had some sales thing in Vegas this weekend."

"Right. And last Friday he called you at work to say he had colleagues visiting from out of town he needed to entertain. And the Friday before that he texted you at work to say he'd just come down with the flu."

"I don't believe this!" she says. "Fine. Next time, I'll make him call you at home so you can hear it from him directly. I'm sick and tired of being the bad guy."

She peels out of the parking lot. We drive all the way to the bank, then the laundromat, in total silence. But by the time we pull into the strip mall parking lot, she doesn't look mad anymore. She looks worried. She reaches over and pulls my ear. She says she knows this has been hard on me. She really will get my dad to call me when he gets back from Vegas. And she's sorry about Chaser Junior; she was just trying to help.

I nod OK. We've got shopping and laundry to do.

The Supa-Sava is mobbed by the time we finally get inside. Mom puts me in charge of driving the cart like nothing ever happened. I don't really pay much attention to what she loads into it. I'm still fuming. I just concentrate on avoiding head-on collisions with little old ladies who are clueless about the rules of the road. Anyway, we're on our way to checkout in record time.

"I think that's it," Mom says.

I make a quick scan of the cart. "What about dog food?" I say.

"Again?" she says. "That dog eats like a horse."

My temper flares right back up. She probably didn't even put dog food on the list. It's like she totally blanks on the fact we have Reggie. You can bet she never forgets her wine, though. I don't have to remind her ten hundred times about that.

"No he doesn't. He eats like a regular dog," I say. "He just needs to eat every day, like you and me."

"Can you please cut me a break with that smart mouth?" she says. "Now give me the cart. I'll go stand at the registers while you grab a can of what we usually get. The lines are going to be murder, and you've still got to run and pull the clothes out of the dryers."

I don't get a can of the usual. Reggie's stomach is fine now. The philodendron incident was a week ago. Instead I pick out the largest bag of dog food I can find. I make sure it's the most expensive brand, with gourmet ingredients. I half drag, half carry the bag to the front of the store.

Oh great. Timmy Burns is standing right there in line in front of Mom. First Chaser Junior, then another spat with Mom, now this. Could my day get any worse?

Timmy's with a man who must be his dad—they have the exact same red hair. They're both loading groceries onto the conveyor belt: frozen pizzas, two-liter bottles of cola, giant bags of nacho chips, jelly donuts, popcorn, bubble gum.

"*There* you are," Mom practically shouts. "I was about ready to send the dogs out after you." If only aliens would abduct me NOW and transport me to their planet in another galaxy. All we've got in our cart is embarrassing stuff like toilet paper, Diet-Rite dinners, and nail polish remover.

"*Shh*," I say.

"What on earth is *that*?" she says, pointing at the bag of dog food.

Timmy and his dad both turn to see what all the commotion is about.

"It'll save us a trip," I say. I can feel Timmy's eyes boring a hole into my skull, but I refuse to look at him.

"And just where do you think we're going to store it?" Mom says. "You know the size of our kitchen. There's hardly enough room in there to change your mind."

"Could you please stop shouting?" I say.

"For Pete's sake," Mom says. She turns to Mr. Burns

and gives him a *What are you going to do?* shrug. He smiles back.

I will all three of them to spontaneously combust.

I hoist the bag onto my shoulder. I step out of line, teetering a little under its weight. I still haven't made eye contact with Timmy.

"*Now* where are you going?" Mom says.

"To get a smaller one," I say.

The bag splits open. To my horror, about ten hundred pounds of dog food cascades to the floor and ping-pongs all over the place.

"Nicky!" Mom gasps.

"*Cleanup at register six!*" echoes the loudspeaker across the whole store.

Timmy bursts into laughter.

I make a beeline straight for pet foods.

"Just get a can of what we usually get," Mom calls after me. "We don't even know how long that dog is staying!"

I take a detour up the sporting goods aisle. I locate the Swiss Army knives. Check. I move on to flashlights. Check. Rain ponchos next. Then a deck of cards . . .

I'm not getting just a can. I'm getting at least a six-pack, or maybe even a case. And I'll be taking my sweet time about it too. Hopefully Timmy and his dad will be long gone by the time I get back. The only good news, I suppose, is that Timmy's going to pulverize me into the ground Monday at lunch recess and put me, finally, out of my misery.

SATURDAY AFTERNOON, UP AT THE MONUMENT,

Sal hands me a Frisbee that's been chewed up by some other dog. Mickey says Sal found it in a trash barrel while he was looking for the sports section to wipe dog poop off one of his bocce balls. It's still perfectly good, Floyd says, except for the teeth marks.

"Thanks," I say. I wonder about what kind of germs it has on it.

"Well?" Sal says.

"Well what?" I say.

"Well, why not give it a whirl?" he says.

"Oh," I say. "OK." I unhook Reggie's leash and hand it to Sal. I look around for cops—they've got signs everywhere saying KEEP OFF THE GRASS and NO DOGS ALLOWED—and then I lead Reggie over to where the old guys play bocce anyway. I show him the Frisbee. I pretend to throw it in slow motion, so he gets the idea. His eyes dart from the Frisbee to my face. That big cartoon question mark appears over his head. I chuck it for real. It flies about three feet and then nose-dives into the grass. Reggie stares at it. I stare at it. The old guys stare at it.

"Try again," Sal shouts.

I try again. It does exactly the same thing.

"It doesn't work," I shout back.

"Of course it works," Floyd says. "It's still perfectly good."

"You're just not doing it right," Mickey says.

Wrong thing to say.

I go mental. I run up to the Frisbee and kick it, kick it really hard. *You're not doing it right.* Basically, what Dr. Holkke tells me every time I sit in his office on Wednesday afternoons—just because I'd rather read stale *Highlights* than role-play or blab all my family business to a total stranger. I jump on the Frisbee and stamp it into the ground. *You're not doing it right.* What Timmy Burns is telling me with his spitballs and threats and locker graffiti—just because I don't know how to dress like a Townie or act like a Townie or play by his stupid Townie rules. I keep jumping on the Frisbee trying to get it to split in half. *You're not doing it right.* Mom at the Supa-Sava this morning about that stupid bag of dog food. Hello, what about buying only one can at a time so she has to go back to the store every single day—is that doing it right? I don't stop wailing on the Frisbee till I'm out of breath. *You're not doing it right. You're not doing it right.*

Reggie watches me the whole time with this sad, worried look on his face. Eventually I calm down. Eventually I head back to the bench for his leash.

"Well, that's no way to behave," Sal says.

"What do you know about it?" I shout. "Have you ever played Frisbee before, you old fart?"

We were supposed to go to Cape Cod on vacation this past Fourth of July. We were going to rent a cottage for a whole week, right on the beach, with a big deck and a barbecue grill. Dad promised me he would teach mc how to throw a Frisbee. And how to sail. How to dig for clams. How to build a bonfire out of driftwood. Maybe even how to ride a horse. Stuff every other kid in Massachusetts already knows how to do. He promised me. It was all planned out. Instead he moved into a motel. Instead Mom put the house on the market. Instead I moved *here* Labor Day weekend.

I don't say another word. I just hook Reggie up to his leash and leave the square without turning back. I'm halfway to Eden Street before my hands stop shaking. I know I should have apologized; those old guys weren't being mean. It was actually pretty nice of Sal to think of me when he found the Frisbee, even if it was used. But sometimes you get sick of apologizing for everything all the time. Sometimes things just get to you after a while. Know what I mean?

LUNCH RECESS, MONDAY. THE SCHOOL PLAYGROUND.

That's weird. I'm halfway through my sandwich, and so far I haven't gotten beat up. Maybe ducking out early on Friday actually did the trick. From where I'm sitting on the swing set, I keep one eye on the kickball game.

The other eye I keep on Rita. I have to admit, she hasn't tried to come over here once to bother me. Instead she's sitting on top of the monkey bars with this other weird-looking, tall girl I've never seen before who's wearing an old-fashioned dress and some really thick glasses. Techni-cally speaking, I owe Rita a thank-you for bailing me out of trouble at my locker. But now she doesn't seem to want to talk to me any more than I want to talk to her.

Some kid pops a foul from one of Timmy Burns's spin pitches. The ball skitters a couple of feet away from me. Here we go.

Timmy comes running over to get it. He doesn't pulverize me, though. He just stands there staring.

"What?" I say.

"You. In the store the other day—with that big-ass bag of dog food."

"Yeah," I say. "So?"

"Hilarious. Thought I was going to piss my pants. Did you do it on purpose?"

Is he *serious*?

"Got a big-ass dog," I say, shrugging. "German shepherd. Purebred. He goes eighty pounds."

"That's, like, more than *you* weigh," Timmy says.

"He's a guard dog," I say. "Trained since birth to protect me."

"Whatever."

"You got a dog?" I say. I don't know what else to say with him, like, standing there not beating me up.

"My mother's afraid of them," he says. "But she's crazy. Your mom's a babe, though."

I can't quite get my head around *that* piece of info.

"That your dad in the store with you?" I say.

"Yeah," he says, rolling his eyes. "He had me for the weekend."

The guys from Timmy's team yell for him to hurry up, he can pick a fight with me later—recess is almost over and they're winning.

"Hilarious," he says again. He runs back to the mound chuckling to himself, and then starts to pitch again.

I take a bite of PB and J. My mouth is so dry I can barely swallow. I take a swig of juice to try and wash it down.

What was that all about?

MONDAY AFTERNOON. THE APARTMENT ON EDEN STREET.

Reading one of my guide-dog books, waiting for Mom to get home from the Ambulance Chasers.

A *babe*? I don't think so.

Reggie shoots me a worried look from where he's parked at my feet. Lately I've only been taking him as far as the strip mall on his afternoon walk. I'm avoiding the monument since the Frisbee incident. I'm also avoiding the butcher shop because of the mailman. It's called lying low, until there's another break in the case.

Here's something interesting: Guide dogs are trained to ignore any command that might place their blind master in danger. It's called intelligent disobedience. When a dog doesn't follow an order, the master knows that he should wait till the coast is clear. Unless the dog is naturally disobedient. Then the dog needs to have a career change.

Is it possible Reggie tried to be intelligently disobedient the day Old Alf stepped off the curb and got sideswiped by the bike messenger? Could Mrs. Strazzulo have just forgotten to tell me that crucial part of the mailman's story—the part that would prove Reggie innocent of any alleged crime? Oh great. Now I *have* to go back to the North End tomorrow, to pump Mrs. Strazzulo for more information. I just hope she doesn't make me buy more meat. She's all about meat.

TUESDAY, AFTER SCHOOL. HANOVER STREET.

I hear your nono's house has a For Sale sign on it," Mrs. Strazzulo says, handing me the usual greasy bundle of bones.

"It does?" I say, then catch myself.

"Mailman says he was delivering at Noyes Place this afternoon while some real-estate guy was putting up the sign. He didn't see your nono around to ask, though."

Noyes Place! Aha!

"I was at school," I say. "My mom must have been at the doctor's with Nono."

"None of my business," Mrs. Strazzulo says. "But that house sure needs a lot of work."

Suddenly I put two and two together. Noyes Place. House that needs work. Reggie's insistence on crossing to the other side of the street.

"So where's he going?" Mrs. Strazzulo says.

Think quick, Nicky!

"Back to California with us," I say.

"That'll be nice for you," she says. "When?"

"You got any pork chops today?" I say to get her off the subject. I don't even like pork chops. It's just the first thing that came to mind.

"How many you want? Four?" Mrs. Strazzulo says. "I've got some nice thick ones."

"Just three today," I say.

She makes out a slip and tucks it under the change drawer in the register. Then she wraps three chops in paper, puts them in a plastic bag, and hands them to me. "Let me know when I should tally up your nono's bill," she says. "He can send you over with a check before he moves out."

I nod and tell her to have a nice night. It's only when we're rounding the corner onto Parmenter that I remember I totally forgot to ask Mrs. Strazzulo more details about what the mailman saw the day of Old Alf's accident.

Jenny is out working in her little patch of garden, so we stop to say hello. She asks what I've got in the bag and I tell her pork chops for dinner. I ask her what she's up to. She says she's trying to pin what's left of the former owner's rosebushes to her newly painted iron fence, but it's really a two-person job. Do I mind helping for a few minutes, since I'm such an old hand in the garden?

I don't see how I have much choice—even though I'm dying to get over to Noyes Place—so I say sure. I park Reggie on the stoop while Jenny sticks the chops in her fridge. She brings back a pair of gloves for me. I hold thorny old vines in place while she ties them to the trellis with twine. Funny, I never did this for Mom back at the old house. I found any excuse not to help her out in the yard.

"Jenny?" I say.

"What, sugar?"

One of those S-and-a-vowel words. "How come you're always alone out here?" I say. It just pops out of my mouth. I swear I wasn't even thinking it.

"What do you mean?" she says.

"Don't you have a husband or anything?"

Jenny laughs. "Nope. It's just me."

"Well, were you ever married?"

"Nope."

"Aren't you lonely?"

Jenny stops working to think my question over. I like that about her—that she takes me seriously, even though I'm only eleven and three-quarters.

"Sometimes. But everyone gets a little lonely sometimes, even when they're married. Mostly I really like living on my own. I get to eat all my favorite foods. I get to watch whatever I want on TV. I get to let the laundry pile up if I feel like it till there's nothing left to wear. Besides," she says, "I'm learning how to play the cello. And I belong to a smart reading group. We do a lot of things together."

"My mom says she likes being on her own," I say. "But she's not very good at it."

"Lucky for her it's only temporary," Jenny says. "Right? I mean, your dad probably can't wait for you guys to get back to California."

He must be back from Vegas. Why hasn't he called?

Suddenly I see my dad walking through the front door of our old house in Littleton, all smiles for a change and totally on time for dinner. It's a Friday night and he's landed a huge order of medical supplies for one of the children's hospitals in Boston, and so his boss has given him a big, fat bonus, plus the whole day off tomorrow. In his hand he has a bouquet of roses for Mom. In his pocket, he has two tickets to the All-Star Wrestling Extravaganza at Boston Garden—one ticket for him, one for me.

"Pork chops are my dad's favorite," I say, out of the blue. "We used to have them once a week back home—in California."

"Mine too," she says. "Especially with a little applesauce on the side."

"Gross," I say. "My dad just likes them plain."

"Will your dad be able to come to Boston for a visit, while you and your mom are looking after your grandpa?"

I consider telling Jenny the same story I just told Mrs.

Strazzulo—that we've put Old Alf's house up for sale, and he'll be moving back to California with us. It's good to keep things consistent. But for some reason, I don't feel up to feeding her one of my usual stories. I wish, suddenly, that I could just tell her the real deal about what I'm actually doing here in Boston.

"No," I say. "My dad has a really stressful job."

"You must miss him a lot," Jenny says.

"What color will those roses be?" I say.

"I don't know," she says. "They'd already come and gone by the time I moved in. We'll have to wait till spring to find out."

We work a while longer. I can smell her perfume. Or maybe it's not perfume, but just the soap she uses. She smells clean and fresh, like she wears clean clothes every day and always washes her hair and never veges out in front of the TV.

"Sometimes."

"Sometimes what?" Jenny says.

Did I really say that out loud? "My mom's garden back home is a lot bigger than this one. We have a gigantic front yard. She grows roses, too, on a trellis. The two of you would like each other."

Maybe when Reggie and I get back to Eden Street tonight, it'll be a good night. Maybe I'll find Mom in the kitchen again, humming and chopping, making up a big pot of macaroni and cheese. Maybe she'll apologize about constantly forgetting to buy dog food at the Supa-Sava. Maybe she'll say Reggie's trial period is officially over and that he's here to stay. Or maybe she'll admit that she was wrong about moving to Boston, that she doesn't want to stand on her own two feet after all. Maybe we'll both raise our glasses of fruit punch and toast to a fresh new start back in Littleton.

"You should have your mom stop by and introduce herself," Jenny says. "Tell her she's welcome to putter around the yard here with me as much as she likes. The two of you could come over for lunch one Saturday."

"I'll ask her," I say.

But of course I won't. Just like I won't actually bring the pork chops home. I'll pretend I forgot them in Jenny's fridge—she likes them. Or I'll feed them all to Reggie on the way over the Charlestown Bridge.

But it would have been nice.

A FEW MINUTES LATER. NOYES PLACE.

Yup, there's a big new For Sale sign on the side of that spooky town house. So it's an official breakthrough in the case. I now know without a shadow of a doubt where Old Alf lives—at least until he sells the place.

"This is your old home, isn't it?" I say to Reggie. "This is where the accident happened."

Reggie yanks at his leash to cross the street. I stand my ground. But before I can climb the stoop and knock on the front door, a yellow cab pulls up to the curb and honks the horn. A moment later, an old man with huge black sunglasses and a long white cane comes out the front door. Instead of a left shoe, he's wearing one of those walking casts. Reggie yelps, and backs his way down the street, pulling me with him. The old man cocks his head and frowns. But then he taps his way down the stoop. He hobbles over to the cab. The driver gets out and tries to take the old man's arm. The old man jerks his elbow away. He gropes for the back door handle. The driver shrugs and climbs in behind the wheel. The old man settles into the back and slams the door. The cab speeds away.

Reggie stops his retreat. He whines and comes over to lick my hand. I tell him it's OK, everything's going to be OK. We cross the street and head for the bridge.

But I'll be back.

TUESDAY NIGHT. AT THE DINING TABLE.

Mom keeps looking over at me. She's pretending to do a stale crossword puzzle from last Sunday's *Globe*. I'm sitting across from her, pretending to do my social studies homework. Secretly, we'd both rather be watching TV.

"What's this?" she says. She's pointing at a big red C+ sticking out of the front of my American history book. Oh great. It's the result of the pop quiz I took on Friday. She pulls out the quiz without even asking and holds it up.

"C-plus?" she says. "You told me you covered the Revolutionary War last year. This should be an A-plus."

Reggie harrumphs from where he's lying under the table.

"I had trouble concentrating," I say. What I don't say: *Because I was too worried about the fake note I wrote to get myself out of lunch recess so I could take a taxi to the pound instead of getting beat up by the school bully.*

"You didn't seem to have any trouble concentrating on the video games you played all weekend."

"The quiz was on Friday," I say. "It was already a done deal."

"That's not the point!" she says.

For some reason, Reggie scrambles to his feet. In the process, he whacks his head on the underside of the tabletop. Mom's wineglass topples over and sloshes a big wet star on my pop quiz.

"Here we go again," Mom says. "Please lock that damn dog in the kitchen."

"It was an accident," I say.

"Do it. You and I need to have a serious talk."

Uh-oh.

I lead Reggie into the kitchen and hand him a butcher-shop bone out of the fridge. I grab the sponge from the sink and head back to the table to face the music.

"It's about Reggie," she says.

"That grade doesn't have anything to do with Reggie," I say, blotting my C+.

"Getting him was a big mistake," Mom says. "He's clearly traumatized by his first owner in some way that causes him to act out. I don't think we can handle the extra stress of that in our lives right now."

"Look," I say. "It's all cleaned up. No big deal."

I try not to panic. I still don't have enough evidence in the Alf Santorello case to clear Reggie's name of any wrongdoing.

"It is a big deal, Nicky. Reggie has driven a wedge between us. He gives you an excuse to avoid dealing with me on some pretty big issues."

"Where'd you get all that?" I say. "The shrink?"

"I don't just sit there in his office like you and stare at the clock."

So ol' Holkke Håkan has been ratting me out to Mom. Supposedly whatever goes on in there is just between him and me. I guess it's official: All grown-ups are in cahoots with each other.

I pack up my homework and stand. I head for the kitchen—the only place I can get any privacy besides the school library.

"God! You're so much like your father it scares me."

I slam the kitchen door on her.

Reggie looks up from his bone. His ears go all flat.

I stand at the fridge, taking deep breaths, trying to calm myself. Swiss Army knife, flashlight, rain poncho, deck of cards . . .

That's the trouble with Mom. She's always trying to get everyone to communicate all the time. It drives people crazy. Next she'll want to talk about what happened that night before the Fourth of July with Dad and the mustard—get all *that* out in the open. Well, too bad. Because if I ever started in on that subject—really spoke my mind for a change—I doubt I'd ever get myself to shut up.

Maybe Dad'll call tomorrow. Maybe he already has.

I take the marker off the magnetized memo board and I draw a big hangman with crazy eyes on the fridge door. Under it I write the words, "I CAN'T TAKE IT ANYMORE!"

I take a few more deep breaths. I grab the little eraser to wipe it all away. Nothing happens. I scrub harder. It's still there. I spit into my palm and rub the fridge door really hard. Nothing. That's when I realize: It's a really old fridge, one that's been painted a couple of times. The marker's not going to wipe away. Ever.

Mom bursts through the door. "I shouldn't have said that—"

I yelp. Reggie yelps.

"What on earth?" Mom says, staring at the fridge.

"Um, we've got a slight problem," I say.

WEDNESDAY AFTERNOON. THE SHRINK.

Dr. Holkke says he'd like to try something a little different today. He appreciates that I may not be much of a talker, not everyone is. Maybe expressing myself verbally just isn't my thing. Maybe I'd prefer to express myself visually. He points to a pad on his coffee table. Next to it are crayons in a ceramic mug.

"You want me to draw a picture?" I say. Is he serious? I'm, like, practically twelve.

"Only if you want to," he says. He's always saying that.

"Of what?" I say.

"Anything," he says. "You decide."

"I'm not too good at art," I tell him. Because I'm not.

"Doesn't matter," he says. "The point is to express what you're feeling and share that with others. Why don't you just start drawing and see where it takes you?"

OK, whatever. Beats sitting around for half an hour. Plus on the drive home I can tell Mom I actually did something here today. Maybe she'll stop giving me the cold shoulder about the fridge, which we're going to have to spray paint white sometime, without the landlord downstairs knowing about it. After we steam clean the carpet, that is.

I draw a big dog with pointy ears. I color the fur brown with big black spots.

"That's a German shepherd," Dr. Holkke says.

Duh!

"Is that your new dog?"

"No." I've never mentioned Reggie to him. But obviously Mom talks his ear off about how that damn dog is driving a wedge between us. Just wait till he hears in a few minutes about how she thinks Reggie caused me to get a C+ in social studies and deface the fridge.

I draw a harness on the dog to disguise him. Only the actual masters of guide dogs get to hold their harnesses in real life. That's how the dogs know it's time to work. When the harness is off, the dog is off duty. Then he can hang out and act like a regular canine: romp with other dogs, get petted by people, play fetch. So technically speaking, Alf Santorello had every right to ask Jenny not to pet Reggie, even though he clearly relaxed the rules with the old guys at the monument. But he obviously unhooked Reggie then, gave him a few minutes off to chase bocce balls.

I need to have a word with this Alf Santorello dude.

The harness I just drew looks sort of stupid floating there in space. So I draw a hand holding it, which looks even weirder, until I attach a whole body to the hand.

"Who's this?" Dr. Holkke says, tapping the blind master with his pen.

"Alf Santorello," I say.

"Who's Alf Santorello?" he says.

I'm dying to say my grandpa. But that whole situation has gotten way out of control.

"Nobody," I say. "I just made him up."

"It's an unusual name," Dr. Holkke says.

Hello, as if Håkan Holkke isn't! "I heard it once, walking around the neighborhood," I say. "I just like the way it sounds."

I add a pair of big black sunglasses to the master.

"Are you sure that's not you, Nicky?" Dr. Holkke says. "The blind guy holding the dog looks a lot like you."

"I told you, it's just some guy."

"Do you know what a metaphor is?" Dr. Holkke says.

"Leave me alone!" I say.

I chuck the crayon I'm holding across the room. It shatters against the wall. "It's just some stupid old man with a stupid dog!" I crumple up the drawing and throw it at him.

We both stare at each other for a full minute.

"Wow," Dr. Holkke says.

"I told you I wasn't any good at art," I say.

WEDNESDAY AFTERNOON. STUCK IN TRAFFIC.

Sitting next to Mom in the front seat feels like one of those gray, rainy days, even though it's actually pretty nice outside. Maybe it's just the gloomy classical music they play before the news on this public radio station.

I sneak a peek at her. She's still staring straight ahead, all stony-faced and silent. When's she going to start yelling at me for losing it in Dr. Holkke's office? He must have told her. He rats me out for saying *nothing*. So far, she hasn't spoken a word to me: not when she was paying up with Holkke's secretary, not when we were walking out to the parking lot, not since we got stuck in rush hour.

"Um, you've got a green light?" I say.

She doesn't hit the gas. She bursts into tears.

Everybody behind us starts honking.

"I'm a terrible mother," she sobs.

Uh-oh. "Maybe you should pull into the breakdown lane," I say.

She nods. She puts her indicator on. She peels off onto the shoulder, nearly hitting an SUV. She slams the car into park.

"There are way-worse mothers in the world," I say.

It doesn't help. She really starts to bawl then.

I turn the radio off. I reach into the glove compartment and hand her a tissue from the packet we've got stowed there.

"Now you're resorting to violence instead of communicating your needs," she says, honking into the tissue. "What's next? Shoplifting? Gangs?"

I think about the Frisbee incident up at the monument.

Then, for some reason, I just say it: "I don't frankly care if you gave me Reggie as some sort of lame consolation prize. And I don't care if Reggie ate your philodendron or spilled your wine. I like him. I like having him around. He makes me feel better. You want me to communicate my needs? I only have one right now. What I *need* is for you to stop threatening to take him back to the pound."

She looks over at me, a little surprised.

"Clear?" I say.

She nods. But she doesn't pull back into traffic. She starts crying again. Oh great. I hand her another tissue from the pack.

"It's been harder than I thought," she says. "Standing on my own two feet. I get into these funks. And when I do, you feel completely unsupported and alone. That's why you drew yourself as a blind kid at the shrink's office today, isn't it?"

Wow. The bottom-line skinny for a change.

"Um, Mom? I'm doing a report on guide dogs for school—remember?"

"Really?" she says. "That drawing was just for school?"

No, not really. I definitely do feel dragged blindfolded around the planet by a bunch of grown-ups who don't know where they're coming from or going to any better than I do.

"Really," I say.

Mom asks for another tissue.

"So we're keeping Reggie right?" I say.

She nods. She throws the car into gear and noses it back into traffic, pissing off about a half-dozen commuters. But at least we're on the road again. She apologizes for freaking out. She says it's just been one of those days—first Chaser Junior about some missing file, then Dr. Holkke with the drawing. How about if she stops by the Supa-Sava? She'll cook whatever I want for supper—to make it up to me. Spaghetti? Macaroni and cheese? Just name it, and she'll get the fixings.

What I really, really want is to hoof it over to the North End and knock on Alf Santorello's door. But I guess hearing what happened between him and Reggie isn't so urgent, now that I get to keep Reggie no matter what. So first things first. Mom just cut me a major break. It's time to cut her one back.

"Thanks," I say, "but it seems like we could both use the night off. How about if we grab Reggie and go for a spin— see a little of Boston for a change? It's a such a nice night out. Maybe we could check out that park along the river that Chaser Junior told us about?"

"OK," she says. "Sure, why not."

A second later we both start laughing like idiots.

LATER WEDNESDAY AFTERNOON. THE ESPLANADE.

Chaser Junior's park actually turns out to be kind of cool. The Esplanade is long and skinny and stretches for miles along the Charles, with these amazing views of the Salt and Pepper Bridge and Cambridge on the other side. There's a paved path all along it for biking and rollerblading. And just like Chaser Junior said, there are playgrounds and a skateboard ramp and even a concert dome called the Hatch Shell. A ton of people are still there when we finally find a parking spot for the car, even though it's almost dusk.

Mom is totally impressed by how well I handle Reggie. When I say, "Forward!" he starts walking. When I say, "Stop!" he stops and sits. Secretly I'm really proud of him. He's proving to her, all by himself, that he's actually a pretty good dog to have around.

We decide to buy a couple of hot dogs and cans of soda for our dinner. There's a snack cart near the Hatch Shell. Near it is a stand with a man selling kites and stuff. We go and have a look while we're eating. A whole bunch of people are flying kites on a little islandlike thing sticking out into the river.

"Which one do you like best?" Mom says.

I point out the kite with a big Superman *S* on it.

"I like that one too," she says. "Let's get it."

I don't say anything.

"What?" she says.

"I don't know how to fly kites," I say.

"Neither do I," she says. "But it can't be that hard, right?"

"We'll look totally lame out there," I say.

"So?" she says. "Nobody knows us around here. Besides, everybody looks stupid flying a kite."

I laugh. She's right.

We cross a little stone bridge to the island and for a few minutes watch how other people are flying their kites. Then we hitch Reggie's leash to the leg of a park bench and give it a whirl. Mom holds the kite steady on the ground while I let out a bunch of string. We wait for some wind. Then I start running while Mom throws the kite up into the air. The first couple of tries don't amount to much. But Mom finally figures out the angle that catches the most wind, and suddenly the kite takes off. It's soaring, and I'm letting out string like crazy. Before you know it, our kite is right up there with the rest of them. Mom comes running over, whooping and clapping her hands. She goes to high-five me. People don't really do that anymore, but she thinks it's still cool, so I go along with it. Like she said, nobody knows us here.

Over by the park bench, I notice Reggie baring his teeth and barking his head off. His hackles are all up, just like that time the Townie teens hassled me.

Maybe he saw a squirrel?

THURSDAY, LUNCH RECESS. IN THE LOCKER CORRIDOR.

I grab my lunch and head for the front doors. I can't say that Timmy Burns and his Townie posse are being nice to me—they're not exactly inviting me to join their kickball team—but they've definitely stopped punching my arm at the recess bell. I guess Timmy can't stop laughing at me long enough to beat me up.

I pass Rita talking to that weird tall girl in the old-fashioned dress. Rita has this panicked look on her face. She's standing with her back pressed against a locker and clutching a science book to her chest. The weird girl is hovering over her, talking a mile a minute. I slow down so I can eavesdrop.

"I told you I can't," Rita says. "I have to babysit Julio."

"Why doesn't your mother just get a real babysitter?"

"We can't afford one," Rita says.

"Well, what about now?" the weird girl says. "We could do it now."

I stop. I turn around. I say, "Hi, Rita, sorry I'm late."

"Oh, hi," she says, a look of pure relief on her face. "I was *wondering* where you were." She points to the weird girl. "Have you met Lulu McFadden? Lulu this is, um—" She draws a blank.

"Nicky," I say. "Nicky Flynn."

"Right. Nicky," Rita says.

"You're the new kid," Lulu says. "I've been meaning to introduce myself."

"You about ready to go, Rita?" I say.

"All set," Rita says. "See you around, Lulu."

Lulu darts a suspicious glance at both of us, then gives up. She says she'll wait for Rita after the final bell, just in case she can get out of babysitting. She scuffles off down the hallway.

"I owed you one," I say.

Rita turns to open her locker.

"Thanks," she says. "Now take a hike."

"How's your baby brother?" I say.

"What's it to you?" she says.

"I don't have any brothers or sisters," I say.

Rita whirls around to face me. "Correct me if I'm wrong," she says. "But didn't you totally blow me off the other day?"

"You were freaking me out. Everywhere I turned, there you were!"

She giggles then—something I'm not expecting.

"I can get pretty intense."

"I'll say."

"Sorry, bro. You looked smart. I guess I just miss smart kids. Most of my friends are at Boston Latin, where I wanted to go. But the commute there would have killed my mom. And with the new baby, she just needs me around right now."

"Oh," I say.

"I promise I'll stop stalking you. *Adiós.*"

"Listen. We may as well eat lunch together," I say. "You don't want that Lulu chick to go postal on you."

She laughs. She pulls the Frisbee out of her locker. "We might even be able to squeeze in a quick game of Ultimate."

I feel my face go red. "I completely suck at Frisbee," I say.

"Not for long, dude," Rita says, spinning the Frisbee on her finger. "All you need is a few pointers, and the doctor is *in.*"

"If it's all the same to you," I say, "I'd rather you show me after school one day. And not on this playground. I'm having a hard enough time fitting in around here."

"So we'll sneak over to Monument Square," Rita says. "It's got great grass."

I still haven't apologized to Sal and Floyd and Mickey for the Frisbee incident. "Signs all over the place say keep off the grass," I tell her.

"So? A bunch of old guys are always playing bocce up there," she says.

I tell her we'd better think of someplace closer. Lunch recess is half over. We end up sneaking onto the front lawn of a church around the corner. It's perfect. The grass there is super-green and cushy—much better, actually, than Monument Square. First Rita shows me what she calls the basic jam, which is the right way to hold a Frisbee, the right motion of the arm, and the right time to release it. When I get that down, she shows me the backhand, the two-finger side-arm, and the thumber. Before long, I'm throwing like a pro. Well, maybe not like a pro. But a heck of a lot better than before. Rita's awesome, though. She can even do some of the tricks you see on those extreme sports shows: the flamingo, the triple fake, even the bad attitude.

On the walk back to school, Rita tells me about her baby brother. Her mom had to take him to a specialist because of his ears. At first they thought it was just an infection. But now they think there might be something wrong with his hearing. He may need an operation to keep from going deaf.

"Where's your dad?" I say, out of the blue.

"Don't have one," she says.

"Oh," I say. "Sorry."

"Why?" she says. "Some kids don't have moms. Others, like you, don't have any brothers or sisters. You just deal with what you're handed, right?"

I tell Rita I have a dog. His name is Reggie, I say, and he's a shepherd. I tell her I really want to teach him how to fetch a Frisbee one day. She takes a pen out of her pocket and writes her cell phone number on my wrist. She says, anytime. If she's not babysitting, let's do it. Dogs who catch Frisbees on the fly are awesome.

THURSDAY AFTER SCHOOL. MONUMENT SQUARE.

I stroll right up to Sal and the other old guys with Reggie. I scan the grass. The Frisbee isn't there anymore. Just bocce balls. Somebody must have picked up the pieces.

"So I lost my cool the other day," I say. "I admit it."

"Forget about it," Sal says.

"You got quite a little temper on you," Floyd says.

"Runs in the family, I guess," Mickey says.

Mickey and Floyd both chuckle.

"What's that supposed to mean?" I say.

"Never mind," Sal says.

"Let's just say the apple doesn't fall very far from the tree," Mickey says, winking at the other two.

They all chuckle this time. Sal reaches in his pocket for his wallet. He pulls out a twenty-dollar bill and hands it to me. "Here," he says. "Go get yourself another one."

"I can't take your money," I say. Frisbees don't cost twenty dollars—even I know that.

"Go on," he says. "All is forgotten."

I say no to the twenty again, but he insists. What else does he have to spend his money on, he says, besides scratch cards? Eventually I take it and shove it in the front pocket of my jeans.

"Bowl a few games with us," Sal says. "You can be Mickey's partner."

"I really need to be getting home," I say.

"Tell your granddad we said hi," Sal says.

"Tell him Mickey said the apple didn't fall very far from the tree," Mickey says. "He'll know what I mean."

I say *See you tomorrow* and command Reggie forward. I've just had this great idea! If I swing by Mrs. Strazzulo's on my way to Noyes Place, I can totally use the twenty to pay off the meat I bought on account—and no one will be the wiser!

Mrs. Strazzulo is shooting the breeze with that mailman when I get there. She spots me through the window before I can get Reggie stopped and turned around. She waves and smiles, and I have no choice but to lead us into the shop.

"This is that grandson of Mr. Santorello's I keep telling you about," Mrs. Strazzulo says to the mailman.

"Funny, I've never seen you around Noyes Place," the mailman says. "I deliver there practically every afternoon."

Steady, Nicky. Keep your cool. You don't want to blow this. Not when things are finally starting to turn around. "School," I say. "Then I walk Reggie."

"Such a nice boy," Mrs. Strazzulo says. "He's taking his nono back to California to live with him."

"California?" the mailman says. "Really? I put a mail-forwarding request through for Alfredo Santorello just yesterday. But it wasn't to anywhere in California. It was to that home for vets, right over in Charlestown."

Oh crap! That's where Sal and Floyd and Mickey live. They're all going to bowl a doubles game of bocce and put two and two together. The jig'll be up then. Then there'll be hell to pay. I'll never be able to show my face around Monument Square again.

"That's just temporary," I blurt out. Shut up, Nicky! Don't make things worse! Get out of there! "Just until my dad finishes building an addition onto our house in California for Nono and Reggie."

"Oh," the mailman says. "Anyway, it's a pity I didn't see him around today, or I'd've said my good-byes. Guess you and your mom are headed home tomorrow, seeing how that's when the mail forwarding starts."

Double crap!

"Um, yeah. Our flight's sometime tomorrow afternoon," I say. "Mom booked the tickets online."

Shut up! Shut up!

"I'd better give you that total on your nono's account," Mrs. Strazzulo says. She rummages around in her register and then hands me a slip of paper. It's way more than twenty dollars. Who knew veal cutlets and a couple of pork chops could cost so much? "You can bring the check by first thing in the morning," she says. "That way I won't have to say good-bye to you now."

I nod and shove the bill into my pocket. When I don't turn up with a check, she'll call the home for vets. Old Alf will tell her he's never heard of me, and then she's going to put two and two together, too. I'll never be able to come back to Hanover Street either. Crap! Crap! Crap!

"I guess I'd better get going," I say. "Mom and Nono need my help packing." I tell Mrs. Strazzulo I'll see her bright and early in the morning. I tell the mailman it was nice to finally meet him. Not! I tell Reggie to go forward.

My only hope is to hoof it over to Noyes Place right now and explain to Old Alf it was all a big misunderstanding about me being his grandson. Hopefully he'll laugh, take the twenty, and work something out with me about the rest of the meat.

As usual, Reggie stops dead in his tracks a few feet away from the stoop.

"Forward!" I say.

He doesn't budge. Classic example of intelligent disobedience. Well, screw the official guide-dog commands. This is an emergency. I drag Reggie, skidding, over to the front steps. He digs his toenails in and refuses to go up. I can't budge eighty pounds of disobedient German shepherd, so I tie him to the railing. Then I march up to the door and ring the bell. I wait. I wait. I wait. No answer. I peek in the letterbox, to see if Old Alf has picked up his mail yet—the mailman said he'd been by. There's still a letter there. I take it out. It's addressed to Alfredo Santorello, all right. The return address says it's from an organization for the blind, with Braille bumps under it.

"Mr. Santorello?"

I peek into the nearest window, but the shade is pulled. All the shades are pulled. I ring the bell again. Reggie flinches. His ears go flat.

"Not a peep," I tell him.

Still no answer. I try the doorknob. It isn't locked.

Reggie begins to growl, really softly.

"*Shh*—" I say, "or heel, or whatever."

I look around. I don't see anyone in the street, so I open the door a crack to peek inside.

An old man in big black sunglasses is standing right there.

I holler and jump back.

Reggie barks.

"What do you think you're doing?" Alf Santorello

says, pointing his long white cane at me. "This is private property and you're trespassing. I'll call the cops!" He's wearing a long black coat and a felt hat, and there are two suitcases on the floor next to the leg with the big plaster walking cast.

"It's OK," I say. "I have your mail." Dumb, I know. But it's the first thing I can think of to get him to stop swinging that cane.

"I don't know you," he says. "Where's the regular mailman?"

It doesn't look like Old Alf has shaved for a while, and his clothes are all stained and rumpled. Plus he smells like pee. I peek past him into his house. It's kind of a mess. Takeout boxes and styrofoam cups are all over the place. That gross smell of rotten food.

"I'm Nicky, Reggie's new master," I say. "We were in the neighborhood, and I thought I'd stop by to introduce myself."

"*That* dog is here?" Old Alf says. "You keep that dog away from me." He steps forward, out onto the stoop. I step back. I don't want him to poke me with his cane. Plus he smells like pee.

Reggie growls louder and bares his teeth. It's that same *Don't mess with me* growl he used with those Townie teenagers. His hackles go straight up like when Mom and me were high-fiving at the Esplanade.

"That dog better not come any closer," Old Alf says,

raising his cane and swiping the air like a sword. "Not if he knows what's good for him."

Reggie yelps. He crouches with his tail between his legs, trembling.

A yellow cab pulls up to the curb and honks three times.

Old Alf lowers his cane. "That's for me," he says. "Now get lost, both of you. And don't ever come back here."

Reggie's on his feet again, and barking like crazy. He looks like he might break his leash. I shove the letter I'm holding into Old Alf's free hand, then scramble down the steps and unhook Reggie from the railing. I don't need to tell him to go forward. We both dash across the street and duck behind a couple of parked cars. Reggie starts to whine, so I clamp my hand over his muzzle. I watch as the cabbie stows Old Alf's bags in the trunk. I watch as Old Alf locks the door and taps his way down the front steps and over to the cab. I watch as the cabbie offers to help him into the backseat and Old Alf jerks his arm away. The cab roars off.

Not only did I *not* get the chance to explain to Old Alf how I was his grandson, but I never even got to ask him what the real story was between him and Reggie. Obviously there're some pretty hard feelings on both sides. Now I'll never know.

I start running again, with Reggie tight to my heels. We don't stop till we get all the way back to Charlestown.

Some detective I turned out to be.

■■■

LATER, THURSDAY NIGHT. EDEN STREET.

We're eating our dinner in front of the TV—or at least pretending to, in my case. I am so totally not hungry. In fact I'm just about to hand my whole plate over to Reggie, who is lying at my feet, when Mom says, "What's the matter? You usually love mac and cheese."

We're half watching a nature show about the habits of wolves. But there's something wrong with the cable signal, and the picture keeps melting.

"Dad call about this weekend?" I say.

She nods. "He said he has some big presentation to make for his boss on Monday. Said he needs to work all weekend. I told him to call you here after four. Didn't he?"

"We've got to move," I blurt out of nowhere.

"Move?" Mom says, standing to fiddle with the remote. "What do you mean, move? You told me yesterday afternoon that you were finally beginning to like it here. We flew kites and everything."

"I told you I liked *Reggie*. I didn't say I liked Charlestown."

I lose it then. I just can't help it.

"I *hate* it here," I say. "This apartment sucks. Charlestown sucks. My school sucks. Dr. Holkke sucks. The Ambulance Chasers suck. Everything sucks!"

Mom and Reggie both stare at me, surprised.

"I want to move back to Littleton!" I say.

"We discussed this when I put the house on the market," Mom says. "I explained to you how important it was for me to put some distance between me and your father. I explained to you that I needed a fresh new start."

"I don't get why you had to break up with Dad at all!" I say.

"Yes you do," she says.

Suddenly there's this picture in my head. I'm back in our old kitchen in Littleton, pretending to read a Dr. Ice comic book at the table while Mom grills pork chops at the stove. Dad storms in from his den with a credit-card statement.

—Your spending is totally out of control, he says to Mom. What's this charge for $175 from the plant nursery?

—It's that new dwarf maple in the front yard, Mom says, taking a sip of wine from the glass perched on the counter next to her.

—The tree that's dead? Dad says.

—It's not dead, Mom says. Just a little traumatized from replanting. It'll come back in the spring.

—Do you think I *like* working twelve-hour days and most weekends so you can plant two-hundred-dollar dead trees in the yard? Dad says. You're driving us to the poorhouse!

—Please don't start yelling tonight, Mom says. Look, I'm making your favorite dinner.

Dad runs his hand through his hair. He picks a jar of mustard up off the counter.

—Twelve dollars? he says, looking at the sticker. Since when does mustard cost twelve dollars?

—It's from France, Mom says.

—Are you out of your mind? Dad yells.

I blink away the tears, snapping my attention back to the TV's pixelated wolves. Both Mom and Reggie are waiting for me to say something. "I bet if you apologized to Dad and really meant it, he'd take you back," I whisper.

"I don't want him to take me back," Mom says.

"Can't you see you've ruined my life?" I say. "Don't you even care?"

Mom takes a deep breath. "This whole thing has been really hard on you," she says. "I totally hear that. But, Nicky, I still believe what I did was for the best. For *all* of us. I need you to try and understand."

I stand up to hit the side of the TV. The pixels disappear. Mom lays a hand on my arm.

"Yesterday, in the car, you told me what your needs were. But you never asked me what I needed."

I don't say anything. I can't.

"I need to feel supported too. By *you*," she says. "Even if you don't agree with every decision I make. It would help to know you're on my side."

When did this conversation get so twisted around?

"So how about a high-five?" Mom says. She raises her hand.

Reggie leaps to his feet. He bares his teeth. His hackles go up.

Mom grabs my arm to pull me to safety.

Reggie goes totally mental.

It all happens in a split second. But it's sort of like time goes into slow motion. Reggie leaps up and knocks Mom over. They both hit the coffee table on the way down. One of the macaroni-and-cheese plates breaks into a million pieces. What's left of my fruit punch glass rolls under the TV, dribbling purple all the way. Mom's wineglass smashes. Next thing I know, Reggie is pinning Mom to the carpet. He's got her wrist in his mouth. He's isn't biting her, but he isn't letting go either. He's just growling that really quiet, really scary warning growl.

The landlord pounds on his ceiling.

All I can think is: There goes the security deposit.

Time speeds back up. I shout at Reggie to get off her. He lets go and sulks over to the corner. I ask Mom if she's OK. She nods. I help her up. I check her wrist. Reggie hasn't left any teeth marks, just a slimy bracelet of slobber. He whines and then takes a few steps toward us.

That's when Mom freaks out.

She pushes me behind her. She grabs her broken wine-glass from the mess on the floor. "Stay away!" she shouts. "Bad dog! Really bad dog!"

Reggie knows he's blown it. Big-time. He backs away. He lies down with his head between his paws. His ears go flat. He sees he's in big-time trouble. He looks really, really sorry.

I take the broken glass out of Mom's hand. She's

shaking. I tell her he didn't mean anything by it. It was just a misunderstanding.

"Don't go near him," she says.

"I'm sure it was a mistake," I say. "Reggie just thought he was protecting me. He doesn't like it when people raise their hands, not even to high-five."

"No," she says. "I knew there was something strange about that dog."

"I swear it's only because he thought you were going to hit me."

"No," she says. "It's in a dog's nature to attack, just like those wolves on TV."

The screen's melting down all over again.

I tell Mom to chill, everything's fine. She says she will not calm down. She has had *enough*. She is the parent, not me, and for once in my life I am going to stop arguing and do exactly as she says. She tells me to put some food in Reggie's dish and set it next to the toilet. After that she wants me to call Reggie over and, as soon as he's eating, lock him in the bathroom for the rest of the night. Above all, I am not to touch him. Do I understand?

I beg her to listen. I start to explain about Alf Santorello and the Pendletons and Reggie's career change but she cuts me off. She says to please, *please*, button it and do as I'm told.

It's been a while since I've seen her like this—not since that awful mustard night before the Fourth of July—but

I know better than to push her any further. I fill Reggie's food and water bowls in the kitchen and then lock Reggie in the bathroom with them. By the time I get back, Mom has cleaned up most of the macaroni mess. "What was I thinking?" she says to herself, scrubbing at the carpet with a sponge. "Look at this place. Look at your clothes. Look at your hair! What the hell could I have been thinking?"

What's wrong with my hair?

I take the sponge away from her. I lead her over to the sofa. She slumps onto it, putting her head in her hands. "He's going back to the pound first thing in the morning," she says. "They can probably come and get him with gloves and nets. They deal with this sort of thing all the time."

"Please don't call the pound," I say, sitting beside her. "Please, Mom."

"NO!" she sobs. "He's going back."

The landlord raps on his ceiling again.

She covers her mouth with her hand. Her eyes fill up with tears.

"*Please*," I say.

"He's going back and that's final," she says. Her voice goes all quiet now—too quiet. "I absolutely refuse to put up with any more violent outbursts in my house," she says. "Ever again."

Dad pounding on my locked bedroom door back in Littleton. Dad apologizing to me from the other side, using his smoothest salesman voice, trying to explain how it was all just a big misunderstanding, how everything's under control now, how he and I should just play a video game while Mom finishes fixing dinner. I can hear Mom somewhere in the background sobbing. I'm huddled in my window seat, peeking out the blinds hoping the neighbors haven't heard all the commotion and are staring out their window at *us*.

I stare at the digitized wolves on TV. Mom tries to put her arm around my shoulder.

I push her away.

She says she needs me to be a little man about this.

"Leave me alone!" I shout.

The landlord pounds even harder.

Mom stands. She wipes her tears away. She finishes cleaning up and shuts herself in her room. I make up the sofa bed. I click through the channels until I find a nature show about Australian dolphins. Supposedly the female dolphins don't get along with the male dolphins very well. The females swim in pods to protect themselves and their babies against roving gangs of males that chase and attack them. That's why dolphins are supposedly so intelligent. The males need to communicate with each other to figure out how they're going to isolate and attack females; the females need to communicate with each other to figure out how they're going to fight off the males and protect their babies. But here's the thing: When the baby dolphins eventually grow up, the females have to push the young males out of their pod. Supposedly the young males don't care; they just swim off to join the nearest male pod.

I can hear Reggie pacing in the bathroom. Every once in a while, he scratches at the door. His high-pitched whine echoes off the shower tiles. But I can also hear Mom sobbing on her bed. So I just watch TV, pretending I'm deaf. Hours go by, seems like. I watch a game show next. I watch a behind-the-scenes show about a rock star from a hair band who became an alcoholic, lost everything, got helped by an angel, and then started singing about it. Mom finally stops crying. I listen while she undresses and shuts off the light. I wait a long, long time, until I finally hear her snoring. Then I tiptoe over to the bathroom door and let Reggie out.

MOMENTS LATER.

He licks every square inch of my face. I tell him to be quiet or we'll get caught. I lead him over to the door and command him to stay. I fish my knapsack out of the closet. I dump everything that's in it—my social studies book, my science book—and try to remember what to pack. Trouble is, I don't actually have a flashlight or rain poncho or Swiss Army knife. I go to the kitchen and stuff a box of Galactic Crunch into the bag. I add my favorite cereal bowl and a spoon. Next I tuck in the two cans of dog food left from our last trip to the Supa-Sava, plus a can opener.

I hesitate. I rip a piece of lined paper out of a notebook I just ditched. I scrawl out a quick note:

Dear Mom,

Reggie is sorry for ~~attacking~~ jumping on you. He just thought he was protecting his Master (me), which is what Man's Best Friend (a dog) always does. The evidence suggests Reggie has had a hard life so far. I think Alf Santorello ~~hit him with~~ didn't treat him very well. I'll explain about him later. But Reggie can't go back to the pound. I know you disagree about this. But I don't think it's right to ditch people (or dogs) you love no matter what the reason is. Especially if it's all a big misunderstanding and they really want to change and said so a million times. If you want me back, it's got to be a package deal. Plus we still need to talk about moving someplace else. Like California. It would be a fresh start for ALL of us. I'll be in touch soon, to find out your answer.

Love, Nicky

I fold the note and stick it halfway under her bedroom door. I hook Reggie onto his leash and lead him out to the front stoop. I have no idea what we're going to do next, but I do know this: Reggie would never attack me. I'm the only friend he's got in the whole world.

"What the heck is going on up there?"

The landlord, standing at his doorway in his pajamas and slippers.

"Oh, nothing," I say. "TV must have been on a little loud."

"Sounded like the battle of Bunker Hill," he says. He points at Reggie. "You better not be roughhousing up there with that dog. That carpet cost twenty-five hundred dollars."

I don't answer. I run for it. Reggie scrambles after me. We don't stop to catch our breath until we reach the end of Eden Street.

Now what?

Reggie starts tugging at his leash. He thinks we're going on our usual rounds. I decide to let him lead me to the monument. Why not? It's as good a place as any, I figure, to wait things out. "Forward!" I say, and we set off in that direction.

A policeman is patrolling Monument Square when we get there. He asks me what I'm doing out so late. I tell him I'm just out walking my dog. He points to the signs that say KEEP OFF THE GRASS and NO DOGS ALLOWED. He tells me to head on home.

"Any ideas?" I say to Reggie, once we're back at the bottom of Monument Ave. He sniffs around a little, whines, and pees on a hydrant. Big help. I suddenly feel like crying again. But I don't. I pull myself together, try to assess the situation. I think of all the places he's taken me: up to the monument, across the Charlestown Bridge, down Hanover Street to Strazzulo's, past Jenny's house . . .

Suddenly I have a plan.

Reggie's not going to like it much. I can't say I do myself. But it's the only thing I can think of. Plus I'm getting cold. My teeth are practically chattering.

We do the normal route until we get to Noyes Place. That's when Reggie figures the plan out. He stops. He takes a few steps backward.

"Come on, boy," I say. "It'll be all right—you'll see. He's gone now. The house is totally empty. There's nothing to be afraid of."

He sits. He stares down at his forepaws. He pretends he's gone deaf. He knows better, I guess.

I have to tug-of-war him the rest of the way to Old Alf's stoop, just like earlier this afternoon. By the time I get him there, he's groaning like crazy and trembling all over. "*Shh*," I say. "You'll wake the neighbors." I try pulling him up the steps by his collar. He flops onto his back, with his feet sticking up in the air. He rolls his eyes at me. He is not going into that house for love nor money.

Plan B, I guess.

I pat Reggie's head. I tell him it's OK, I understand. I tell him to be a good boy and wait for me, right there at the bottom of the stoop—I just need to get warm for a few minutes. I don't bother with tying him up. He's not going to ditch me.

I try the window next to the front door. It slides up a couple of inches and gets stuck. I push it a little harder. Old paint comes flying off the casing like a mini snowstorm, but the window only goes up about another inch or so. This time I give it a really hard shove. Reggie huffs at this—a short, whispery sort of bark—so I stop. Anyway, there's just enough room now for me to squeeze through.

"Not a peep," I say to Reggie.

I take the window headfirst, like I'm in a slow-motion dive. Well, not really. I get a little stuck halfway and have to flatten my rump to wiggle it past the windowsill. I land with a thud in the front hallway. Marky would think this was fun. And maybe it would be if he were here. Then again, I wouldn't be in this mess to begin with.

It's pitch-dark because all the shades are drawn. I tug on the one over the window I've just crawled through. It rattles up and I jump about a foot. Outside, Reggie starts to whine. I take a couple of deep breaths to calm myself. I poke my head back through the window and *shh* him.

Now there's enough of an orange glow from the streetlamps, and I can sort of make out what's what. Directly in front of me is a staircase, which must go up to the second floor. Through the archway to my right is a dining room; through the one to my left is a living room. All the furniture is really old and worn-out, and everything is coated in about an inch of dust. Pizza boxes, styrofoam containers. Plus that funny smell, like rotten food or a dead mouse.

"Mr. Santorello?" I say—not too loud.

No answer.

"Mr. Santorello, are you there?"

Nothing.

I take a step toward the living room. It's really dark beyond the archway. I freeze. Is that a man sitting there? No, it's only an empty armchair.

"Alf?"

There's a scratching noise at the front door. This time I jump about two feet. Get a grip, Nicky! It's only Reggie. He must have sneaked to the top of the stoop after all.

I go and unlock the door, open it a crack. "What?" I say.

Reggie hangs his head and groans.

"Well, what's it going to be?" I say. "In or out?"

He hesitates a second. He groans again. Then he slinks in.

So it's back to Plan A.

Reggie turns his head right and sniffs. He turns left and sniffs again.

"OK?" I say.

He sneezes.

Together we sneak into the living room. Reggie stops suddenly. The hackles on the back of his neck go up. I look where he's looking. There's a framed photo on a side table next to the sofa. It's of Old Alf standing next to a dark-haired woman Mom's age. I go over for a closer look, but Reggie makes that scary low growl again. "It's OK, boy," I say. I reach for the photo. Reggie bares his teeth. I stop. "It's just a picture," I say. He looks like he's going to start barking, so

I turn it facedown on the table. Reggie stops growling. He sniffs the air again. He sits and begins to pant.

I open the living room blinds. Yikes, is it cold in here! I go into the dining room and take the tablecloth off the table. I bring it back to the living room and shake it out.

Reggie watches my every move.

On the sofa, I make a sort of sleeping bag out of the tablecloth. I crawl inside and arrange some of the sofa cushions around me. Then I coax Reggie to climb up onto the sofa. He's not happy about it, but he does eventually. He circles twice, whines, sniffs the air. Finally he settles at my feet. I pet him and cover him with some of the tablecloth. I tell him to get some sleep, we've got a big day tomorrow. I lie back and close my eyes.

Boy, what a mess I'm in right now.

I can hear all the noises the house is making. Like somebody tiptoeing around upstairs. Like somebody rattling a key in the back door.

There's no way I'm going to sleep. I roll onto my side and try to wipe my mind clear. Pretend you're playing one of your video games, Nicky. Pretend you're listening to a decent hip-hop station on the car radio. Or drawing a picture.

I draw a pretend picture on the insides of my eyelids.

I'm at the Esplanade, on that island with all the kites near the Hatch Shell. I'm tossing a Frisbee to Reggie. The Frisbee's brand-new and slices through the air like a flying saucer. Reggie is streaking along beneath it. He leaps up and snatches it out of the sky. He makes a perfect four-point landing with it clenched between his teeth. Then he trots back to me, smiling. They're all cheering behind us: Sal and Floyd and Mickey sitting in lawn chairs, Mrs. Strazzulo grilling up pork chops and cutlets at a portable barbecue grill, Jenny and Mom setting a picnic table. Rita's there, cheering me on from the sidelines. Even Marky's there, because he's visiting me in Boston for the weekend.

My dad is there too.

He's the one clapping the loudest of all. And it's Dad who comes strolling over to put his hand on my shoulder real gentlelike and say, *Nice going, Nicky. That was really good. I'm proud of you. You too, Reggie.*

PART TWO

IN THE DOGHOUSE

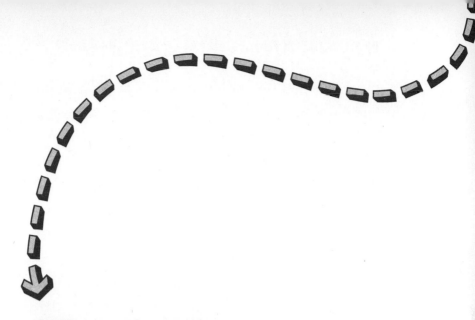

FRIDAY MORNING. BUT WHERE AM I?

I sit up wondering if I've really run away or if that was just part of the bad dream I was having. Sure enough, this isn't my sofa, but Alf Santorello's lumpy old plaid one. And covering me isn't my faded Dr. Ice comforter but a greasy tablecloth.

Where's Reggie?

I feel a little better as soon as I see him standing guard at the front door. I'm not completely alone. At least we're in this together. "Attaboy!" I say. He scratches at the door and whines. Don't blame him one bit. This place gives me the creeps too.

I pull on my shoes. I slip my knapsack over my shoulders. I take the tablecloth back to the dining room. On the way, I notice a half-open closet in the entryway. I peek inside. It's pretty much empty, except for whatever's jangling on the back of the door. A leather harness! Reggie starts wagging his tail when he sees it. It must be his official guide-dog uniform. I stuff it into my knapsack. I let Reggie out onto the front stoop and set the knapsack at his forepaws. I tell him I'll be right back. I step into the front entryway to lock the door from the inside. When I crawl out the little side window, I make sure to leave it open a crack—just in case.

I take five great big gulps of fresh air. Boy does it feels good to be out of that pee-smelling dirty house, even if we have nowhere else to go.

I wish Alf Santorello really was this nice old man who got mugged by a roving gang of BMX-riding Townies in spite of his faithful guide dog's best efforts. I wish his daughter— the woman in the photo—and his grandson, not pictured, had come out from California to take care of him. I wish his grandson had kept him company by playing Monopoly and reading him books. And I wish it really was his grandson's job to walk Reggie every afternoon to keep him in tip-top shape. Wouldn't it be nice if Old Alf decided, once he got better, to move to California and live at his daughter's house? Reggie would be living in California right now. He and Alf's grandson would probably be strolling beneath the palm trees on Reggie's day off, checking out the Avenue of the Stars.

But that's not what the evidence suggests.

When you piece together all the clues, the evidence

suggests Alf Santorello is a mean old guy with big black sunglasses who smells funny and always wears the same stained clothes. Someone who's always losing his temper about something, yelling for no good reason at nice women like Jenny who just want to give his dog a little scratch behind the ears. The evidence suggests he raised that long white cane of his and hit Reggie with it whenever he couldn't find anyone else to blame for mixing up his guide-dog commands. Which is probably why Reggie now has a bad hip. Which is also why Reggie freaks out whenever anyone—like Mom—raises a hand, even to high-five over getting a stupid kite up in the air. It's probably also why Old Alf's daughter lives as far away from him as she can get. She's afraid he'll lose his temper with her, or worse, with her son. In fact, it probably got so bad that Reggie said to himself, *Enough is enough!* and let his master step out into the street while a bicycle messenger was zipping past. Which is probably why Old Alf fired him and brought him back to the training school. And now Old Alf has no one, not even his daughter, not even his not-pictured grandson, which is why his place is a mess, because he couldn't take care of himself with a broken ankle, and why he decided to sell it and move to that home for vets.

Forget about it, Nicky. You got your own problems right now.

I hook Reggie onto his everyday leash. Looks like it's going to be another sunny fall day outside. TGIF. Yeah, right. Reggie starts tugging me in the direction of the Charlestown Bridge. "Stop!" I say. He stops and sits. I kneel down beside him, so that we're facing each other eye-to-eye. "Charlestown's off-limits," I tell him. "At least until Mom chills out a bit." He licks my chin. Trouble is, a lot of places are off-limits today: Monument Square, Hanover Street, my school . . . "We're just going to have to find someplace new to hang out," I say.

Boy, do I gotta pee. (I was way too freaked out last night to do any exploring at Old Alf's place.) So the first stop is the nearest park or public restroom . . .

And suddenly I get this really great idea.

A LITTLE LATER. PAUL REVERE'S HOUSE.

Remember this?" I say, pointing down at the red-brick line in the sidewalk. "It's the Freedom Trail." Reggie cocks his head and his usual cartoon question mark appears between his ears. "Let's just follow it for a while," I say. "See where it takes us." Reggie looks back toward Hanover Street. "Not in that direction," I say. "Into Boston. You and I have never really been there much, except for that time we went kite flying at the Esplanade." I skip mentioning the time he ended up at the vet to have the philodendron pumped out of his stomach.

The red-brick line leads us out of the North End to this

brand-new park they've built over what they call the Big Dig. Supposedly they've dug a tunnel right beneath our feet so that all the honking and beeping of the traffic jams on I-93 can happen underground, where nobody will hear it. That said, Reggie and I still have to put up with a fair amount of honking and beeping from cab drivers *above*ground as we cross Atlantic Avenue and follow the red-brick line into the park. We wind our way through a bunch of ugly new sculptures—modern art, supposedly—till we finally get to a super-nice area called Quincy Market on the other side, where there are all sorts of shops and restaurants—and a restroom. Dad and I ate lunch here that day we did the Freedom Trail, in a gigantic food court in Faneuil Hall. It was here where, supposedly, the patriots met to plan how they were going to revolt against England and form their own country. Dad told me I could buy whatever I wanted from whichever stall, something Mom would never let me do. So I had not one but *two* hot dogs called Fenway Franks, named after the ballpark where the Red Sox play, because that's what they eat, I guess, in between innings. Dad had New England clam chowder served in a bowl made out of sourdough bread. We sat on a stone bench outside so we could people-watch as we ate. Dad promised to take me to a Red Sox game sometime, if they were ever on a winning streak again.

I wonder if he really is working all weekend, like Mom said.

After a quick pee, I find the exact same stone bench and

lead Reggie over to it. I take off my knapsack and fish out the box of Galactic Crunch. I open a can of Reggie's food and empty all of it into my cereal bowl. I know he should only be getting half, but what am I going to do with the rest? I eat handfuls of cereal out of the box while Reggie licks the bowl clean. Together we watch all sorts of grown-ups in business suits rushing off to their offices with cups of coffee in their hands. To our left, a street performer dressed half like a patriot, half like a clown pulls a bunch of balls out of his duffel bag and starts juggling.

Maybe Reggie and I could become street performers. Reggie's been looking for a career change. If I perfect my flamingo, triple fake, and bad attitude, we might be able to travel across America giving Frisbee exhibitions until we get to California.

Before you know it, the cereal box is empty.

"Come on, boy," I say, throwing it in the nearest trash can. "Let's see what else is on this trail o' freedom."

The red-brick line leads us across a couple of busy streets and into a cobbled square where there's an old-looking brick building. I check the plaque so I can tell Reggie why it's there. "This is the Old State House," I say. And then I remember most of the story from the first time around. "They had something called the Boston Massacre here. King George of England got mad at the patriots for revolting, see, so he sent a bunch of redcoats over to teach them a lesson. But that cheesed off all the patriots who were hanging out in front

of the king's royal headquarters in Boston—this very spot—
so they started calling the redcoats names, which caused the
redcoats to fire their muskets at them, which only cheesed the
patriots off even more." People come pouring out of the brick
building's basement. "As soon as the patriots formed their
own country, they decided to build their own statehouse," I
explain to Reggie. "So they turned this one of the king's into
a subway station. See? There's the sign for the T."

Dad and I rode the T that day we did the Freedom Trail,
from Park Street to North Station, where we had tickets to
see the All-Star Wrestling Extravaganza at Boston Garden.

Up ahead on the brick line, a bunch of sailors in white
uniforms are arguing over a map. One of them points the
way, and they all move off. "Let's follow them," I say to Reggie.
He and I could join the navy, if all else fails. On TV, they're
always looking for help. I could even ask to be posted on Old
Ironsides. The naval officer who gave Dad and me our tour
told us half the crew were orphan kids back in the day. Plus
they always had at least one dog on board to catch rats.

Eventually we all end up at the Old South Meeting
House. Reggie and I don't step inside with the sailors
because—sorry—churches are boring. Instead Reggie
and I wind our way through a maze of department stores
to a spooky-looking cemetery called the Granary Burying
Ground. I don't take Reggie through the gates, even though
loads of other people are wandering around looking at the
tombstones sticking up out of the grass like broken teeth.

This stop on the Freedom Trail totally gave me the creeps the last time. Plus I don't want to risk Reggie lifting his leg on Mother Goose, who is supposedly buried there. So I just tell Reggie about it from the sidewalk, cribbing from the plaque. "This is where all those patriots from the Boston Massacre got buried," I say. "Plus Paul Revere—remember him? From the midnight ride?—and Samuel Adams, the guy, I guess, who must have invented Quincy Market, where we had breakfast."

Suddenly a big purple truck roars past. Everybody inside shouts, *Quack! Quack!* Reggie's ears go all flat, but I tell him it's OK. "That's a duck boat," I say. "They go on both land and water. The kids in homeroom were telling about it." I look down the street where it came from. There's another white duck boat at the corner of a big park. We watch some people get off, others get on. "Look," I say. "That must be a stop on the tour. Let's check it out!"

We hoof it over there. Turns out, the park is actually Boston Common, where in the olden days you were allowed to graze your sheep for free because it belonged to everyone. The white duck boat is parked at the entrance to a subway station. It's Park Street, the same one Dad and I used to take the T to the wrestling show. Standing next to the gangplank is the duck boat's driver. He's dressed all in white and wearing a white wig like some sort of patriot ghost. He's put out a sandwich board and is selling tickets. Kids under twelve have to pay twenty dollars, but it's a lot more for grown-ups. Too bad I don't have any money—Wait! I do! I have that twenty-dollar bill Sal gave me for the Frisbee! I reach in my pants pocket to check and, sure enough, there it is. Forgot all about it, what with all the commotion.

"One, please," I say, stepping up with Reggie. "I'm under twelve." It's the first time I've *ever* felt glad to say that.

"No dogs allowed on the tour," the driver says.

Think quick, Nicky.

"But he's a professional guide dog," I say. "You have to let them go everywhere." I know that from my research at the library.

"Too bad you're not blind," he says. "Disabled tickets are half-price. Now beat it, kid. Next!"

Reggie and I step aside. A couple more people buy tickets. The driver folds up his sign and climbs behind the wheel. The white duck boat roars off with everyone shouting, *Quack! Quack!*

I lead Reggie over to a nearby park bench and take a seat. Behind us is the new statehouse, which I don't even bother to point out to Reggie. We've walked a really long way, and I'm kind of pooped. Plus I'm getting a little nervous about Reggie's hip, now that free bones are a thing of the past.

I spy a dollar store across the street and get another good idea. I hitch Reggie's leash to the bench and tell him to stay. Inside the store, I look for the sunglasses rack. When I find it, I pick off the biggest, blackest pair. I bring it over to the checkout counter and lay down my twenty.

"Two dollars," the lady says.

"It's called a dollar store," I say. "That's false advertising."

"Says two bucks right on top of the rack," she says.

I don't argue. I've got a boat to catch.

"Need a bag?" she says.

"No," I say. "I'll wear them out."

I pull Reggie's harness out of my knapsack when I get back to the bench. "Sorry about this," I say. "I know you're retired, but it's an emergency." He doesn't seem to mind. In fact, he's really into it. By nudging me with his head, he sort of shows me how to put the harness on him. I pack his regular leash away and I take hold of the harness handle. I straighten the sunglasses on my nose.

Just in time. A yellow duck boat pulls up in front of the T station.

"Ready?" I say. Reggie stands at attention, waiting for my command.

"Forward!" I say.

LATER FRIDAY MORNING. PARK STREET STATION.

I hand my ten-dollar bill to the driver. This one's dressed in a yellow-feather duck suit with yellow tights and a yellow duck-billed baseball cap.

"Um, where are your folks?" he says.

"They're doing the Freedom Trail," I say. "Way too

many churches for my taste, so I decided to take the duck boats instead."

"I'm not sure that's such a good idea," he says. "In case you need any help."

"That's what my guide dog is for," I say.

"What's the holdup?" some guy in a Red Sox cap calls down from the front seat of the boat. "Let's get this show on the road!"

The driver checks his watch. "Fine," he says to me. "But I'm warning you, I'm not allowed to make any special stops."

Like where?

He grabs my arm and starts dragging me up the steps of the boat—until Reggie makes that low warning growl of his.

"Easy, boy!" the driver says, throwing up his hands like he's under arrest.

"He doesn't like it when people grab me," I say. And neither do I, frankly—especially grown men dressed like big yellow birds. "We can handle it on our own," I say.

"Sue me for trying to help," the driver says, climbing up into the boat and taking his seat behind the wheel.

"He probably will," the Red Sox guy says, laughing.

Reggie and I climb aboard. I make a big show out of groping for the handrail, while staring straight ahead. But I'm totally peeking behind those big black sunglasses—just in case.

"You're going to have to move," the driver says to the Red Sox guy. "That front seat is reserved for the handicapped."

The word is *disabled*, not *handicapped*. Even I know that.

"I paid my money fair and square," the guy says. "There's an empty seat right behind me. The kid won't mind. It's not like he's going to miss a whole lot."

Why are they both shouting? I'm supposed to be blind, not deaf. And why are they talking *about* me rather than to me?

"The empty seat is fine," I say.

God, what blind people must go through! For a split second I consider closing my eyes, just to see. But I chicken out. I tell Reggie to go forward. Without even hesitating, Reggie scrambles over to the empty seat behind the Red Sox guy. He wedges himself between my legs as soon as I'm settled. Pretty impressive, I've got to admit. With the harness on, Reggie is super-confident, super-serious, super-alert— the real deal. There's no way Old Alf could have retired him just for screwing up on the job, like Mrs. Strazzulo's mailman claimed.

"*Now* are we finally ready?" the driver says.

"About time," the Red Sox guy mutters, crossing his arms.

I can barely see anything, he's so fat.

The driver fires up the engine. We all shout, *Quack! Quack!* and roar off toward the burial ground. The driver pulls alongside the fence and switches on his microphone.

He tells us all about it—basically proving I was right. Before you know it, we're also passing the Old State House and Quincy Market again. Since these are sights we've already seen, I let myself zone out a little. There's a man wearing a cowboy hat across the aisle. Maybe, once Reggie and I get to California, we can sign on as ranch hands someplace. Reggie could round up dogies and I could help herd them back to the corral on my trusty palomino. Learning how to ride a horse was one of the things I planned to do on Cape Cod this past Fourth of July before, well—

All the fireworks.

We're on the McGrath/O'Brien Highway now, the road Mom and I take to Dr. Holkke's office. The duck boat stops at the Museum of Science to let more people off and on. According to a banner outside, they've got a big mummy exhibit going. That's another thing Reggie and I could do, I bet: work on one of those archeologist digs. I was way into dinosaurs last year, in fifth grade, and Reggie would definitely like the bones.

Suddenly there's a ramp straight ahead that disappears into the muddy green water of the Charles River. The driver tells us to hang on to our hats, and he guns the engine. We plunge right in, spraying water on everyone. Reggie's ears go flat—clearly he doesn't think this is all that fun—but I quack with the best of them as we pass through a canal and start chugging along the shoreline of the Esplanade.

The driver asks if any of the kids on board want to take

a turn at driving the boat. The only other kid my age waves his hand and makes his way down the aisle. I'm dying to have a turn. But I keep my hand down. It would totally blow my cover to drive since, in theory, I can't see. If I became a duck boat operator, though, I'd get to steer one of these bad boys every single day. And I'd for sure bend the rules and let anybody's dog on. Because Reggie would be sitting right up front with me, navigating.

Don't know about the feather duck suit, though.

Eventually the driver turns us around and we head back up the boat ramp, gushing and dripping water. Uh-oh. We're crossing the bridge that goes straight into Charlestown. I watch in horror as we pass the community college, then the Supa-Sava strip mall. Sure enough, the driver takes a right onto Warren and a left onto Monument Ave. Before you know it, we're pulling up in front of the old guys playing bocce.

And there's Old Alf himself, looking a lot more cleaned up, getting ready to throw a red ball.

Luckily, a bunch of people are getting off. "Let's go," I whisper to Reggie. I try to camouflage us as tourists at the end of the line. But the second we step off the boat, Mickey points over and says, "Hey, isn't that what's-his-name with Reggie?"

"Run!" I say to Reggie.

He doesn't. There's an oncoming car. He's totally blocking my path. "I'm serious," I say. "This is an emergency!" He doesn't budge.

Old Alf shouts for me to get over there. He needs a word with me.

I don't know what comes over me then, but I turn and start yelling at him: "You just didn't know the right commands! I bet he tried to warn you about the bike messenger, but you wouldn't listen! It's not Reggie's fault you're blind and cranky about it! You had no right taking it out on him! You don't deserve him!"

Reggie yanks hard on the leash. The coast is clear now. We both hightail it down Monument Ave. We only stop to catch our breath once we reach Warren. "Boy, that was close!" I say. "Why didn't you just dodge traffic?" Reggie licks my hand, as if to say *Sorry!* I shuck him out of his work harness and stow it in my knapsack. I give him a little hug, though, before hooking him onto his regular leash. He was, after all, on duty.

Suddenly I'm starving.

I check my watch. It's way past my lunchtime. I count out how much money I have left from the twenty. There's probably enough for a taco or two. I head Reggie in the direction of the strip mall.

FRIDAY AFTERNOON. TACO MUCHO.

There's a big sign on the front door I never noticed before: NO DOGS ALLOWED. It also says NO SHIRT, NO SHOES,

NO SERVICE. I've got all those other things covered, but I'm not leaving Reggie outside.

I decide to walk through the drive-thru.

At the little order speaker, I ask for two loaded Taco Grandes, a plate of Nachos Supremo with extra cheese sauce, and a large Lime-O-Lada. The lady's voice at the other end of the speaker tells me how much it's going to be. I cancel the nachos. She gives me the new total and says, "Will that be all, ma'am?" I swallow my pride—I gotta work on lowering my voice—and ask for an extra cup of water, which I know is free. The lady says, "Thank-you-drive-through."

Reggie and I stroll over to the pickup window. I hand the lady the money. She gives me and Reggie an *I don't think so* look. I can see my food's right there, but she doesn't seem like she's planning on handing it over.

"Can I have my change?" I say, adding "*Por favor*" just in case she's Latina. But my accent isn't anywhere near as good as Rita's.

"I thought you sounded a little young," she says.

"Is there a problem?" I say.

"This drive-thru is for cars," she says.

Obviously.

"My mom sent me down here," I say. "She's too busy packing to make lunch. We're moving to California today."

I can tell the lady doesn't believe me. She thinks I'm skipping class, which of course I am.

"Next time order inside," she says. She pushes my stuff

through and rings me up, then hands me back my change. Wow, there isn't much left. Twenties sure don't go very far these days.

"OK," I say. "*Gracias.*"

She rolls her eyes. "Welcome to Taco Mucho," she says into her headset to the car pulling up behind me.

Whatever. There isn't going to be a next time.

I take everything over to one of the picnic tables at the front, where she can't see me. I wolf down the first taco while Reggie watches. I really shouldn't open another can of dog food for him—that vet said only one per day on account of his weight—but I feel bad and give him half of the second taco. I take the lid off the water and let Reggie lap out of the cup while I drink my Limo-O-Lada. Then I just sit there, wondering how in heck I ended up broke and right back in Charlestown.

I notice Rita's cell phone number on my wrist. It's a little smudged, but I can still read it. I take one of the quarters left in my pocket and go to the pay phone by the front door. I dial the number. I wait six or seven rings for her to answer.

"Who's this?" Rita says.

"It's Nicky," I say.

"Better make it quick, bro," Rita whispers. "I ducked out of science lab pretending I had to go to the bathroom."

"Sorry," I say. "It's sort of an emergency."

"You weren't at lunch recess," she says. "You sick?"

"I ran away from home," I say.

"Shut up!" she says. "Why?"

"Remember I told you I had a dog named Reggie? Well, he and my mom got into a big misunderstanding last night," I say. "Mom threatened to send him back to the pound and I took off."

"Ouch," Rita says. "That's not good."

"Listen, do you have any money on you?" I say. "I'm down to pocket change and I don't know how long it's going to take Mom to chill out."

"Not much," Rita says. "But maybe I can ask Lulu McFadden."

"I'll meet you on the playground after school," I say.

"Not that we're friends or anything," she says, "but I really think you should work things out with your mom ASAP. You ever seen any of the homeless kids hanging around the Public Garden? It ain't pretty."

"I'll bear that in mind," I say.

"Oops! Mrs. Johnston at ten o'clock," Rita whispers. "Gotta go! Meet you on the playground at the final bell."

She hangs up.

"*Gracias, amiga*," I say, even though I know she's not there.

FRIDAY, 2:45 P.M.
OUTSIDE THE SCHOOL GATES.

I scan the second-floor windows, trying to figure out which window is *my* window, the one I look out of from the library. My carrel still has all of my books and papers and stuff in it. Mr. Gilmore made me do an outline for my independent study, and that's there too. It's what I'd be working on this very minute, if things hadn't gotten so out of hand.

The final bell goes off. Kids start streaming out the doors.

"Hey!" someone shouts. I look over. It's not Rita. It's Timmy Burns. He's pointing at me. Behind him are Chris McDuff and Johnny Hedges.

Should have figured his sense of humor would wear off.

"Run!" I say to Reggie, forgetting the official command.

We run as fast as we can. I don't look back till we're safely around the corner of the next block. While I catch my breath, I keep an eye peeled, in case they're following us. They're not. But they're probably lurking around the playground, waiting for me to come back so they can finally beat me up—which I totally don't need right now. So much for meeting Rita. I could really have used whatever money she might have scrounged up from Lulu McFadden.

Now I don't have much choice. I have to try and patch things back together between Reggie and Mom. May as well go back to the apartment and wait for her to get back from the Ambulance Chasers.

"Forward!" I say. "Take us home." Reggie sets off in the direction of Eden Street. He's already learned that "home" means the apartment in Charlestown, not Alf Santorello's house in the North End. That makes me feel sad. He doesn't even realize Charlestown isn't home for me. At the moment, there's no such thing as home.

A FEW MINUTES LATER. EDEN STREET.

Uh-oh.

A police cruiser is double-parked in front of our building. Two officers stand at the bottom of our stoop with Mom. She's talking the ear off one of the cops—showing him how tall and wide something dog-size is with her hands—while the other one reads the note I slipped under her bedroom door last night.

"Stop!" I say to Reggie. "About-face." We head in the opposite direction before any of them looks up. Time for Plan C, I guess. Mom must really have it out for Reggie if she's getting the cops involved.

Now we really *are* running from the law.

JUST AFTER DARK. NOYES PLACE. AGAIN.

Back to crawling through the open front window of Old Alf's empty house. (We've hung around the neighborhood for what seems like ages—until most of the neighbors have gotten home and settled into their suppers.) As soon as I land with a thump inside, though, I realize something's different. The blinds are up, so I can see pretty well. All the pizza boxes and styrofoam containers are gone. The floors are spotless. The whole place smells like pine cleaner.

"Is anybody there?" I say. All I hear is the echo of my own voice. Whoever cleaned up has come and gone. Then I remember that that's what you do when you're selling your house. You make it seem like nobody has ever lived there.

Reggie scratches at the front door.

I unlock it and let him in. I kneel down to have a word with him. "Don't worry," I say. "We won't be here long. We're just lying low for an hour or two while I figure out what to do."

He sticks his tongue in my ear.

"Gross," I say, but it makes me feel a little better. Because I feel totally weird breaking back into Old Alf's house now that I've yelled at him.

"So where's the bathroom in this joint?" I say to Reggie. "I gotta pee again."

I open the first door down the hall leading off the entryway. Reggie follows tight at my heels. It looks like a little office. I try the next door. A bathroom—psyched! I don't usually leave the bathroom door open, but Reggie doesn't seem to want to leave my side. It creeps me out a little that he's watching me lift the lid and do my business. Then again, I watch him go all the time. When I'm done, I flush. The whoosh seems really loud—like, loud enough for the neighbors to hear—which freaks me out—maybe I should have just left it. Or maybe flushing is always that loud and I've never noticed before. I don't wash my hands at the sink, just in case. Instead I peek in the medicine cabinet. Empty. That makes me want to check the cabinet under the sink. Also empty, except for a few cleaning products. No towels on the rack, no toilet paper in the dispenser, no soap in the dish. There is a bathroom scale beside the toilet, though. I stand on it.

"Eighty-two pounds," says a computer voice.

I jump back, trying not to laugh. I step just one foot back on.

"Forty-four pounds," it says.

I wonder what other gizmos Old Alf left behind.

I go back to the little office. Every drawer and shelf and cupboard is marked with a Braille strip, and there's even a Braille calendar on the desk. Way in the back of the top drawer, I find a plastic wallet with individual sleeves for keeping all the different kinds of bills separate. No money, though. I also find a deck of Braille playing cards and, best of all, a talking compass. I stuff these last two things into my knapsack, just in case.

At the end of the hall there's an old *I Love Lucy* kitchen. Reggie scoots past me to the back door and scratches at it. I raise the shade and peek out. A small yard surrounded by a high wooden fence. On the right side, there's a gate opening onto an alleyway that must lead to the street. Old

Alf couldn't have been much of a gardener. There aren't any nice trees or bushes or flowers back there. In fact, there's barely any grass. Just mounds and mounds of dried-up dog poop. Poor ol' Reggie. No wonder he likes Monument Square so much. He whines and scratches again. Fair's fair, I guess. I open the door just enough for him to squeeze through. "Be quick about it," I say. He sniffs twice around the yard before he finds a fresh spot. As soon as he does his business, he comes back. Good boy.

All the knobs and buttons on the stove have Braille stickers. Each of the cooking rings has a funny-looking guardrail around it—so you don't burn your hand by mistake, I guess. Every cabinet door is also labeled with a plastic Braille strip. I open them all up. The plates and cups and silverware are still there and they're all normal. But the food cabinets have been emptied out, except for crumbs and a few toothpicks.

There's a set of five canisters on the counter. I peek inside one. Nothing. Then I notice the lids all have two buttons labeled in Braille: one big black one and a smaller red one beside it. I press a black button.

"Tea bags," the canister says—not in a computer voice, but in a real man's voice—Alf Santorello's voice.

Reggie starts barking.

I drop the lid. I wheel around and clamp my hand over his muzzle. "Shh!" I say. "Are you crazy?" He backs away, grumbling. I let him go. I'm dying to press all the other buttons, but I'm afraid Reggie will go mental. I pick up the lid I've dropped and press the little red button. Nothing happens, except a hissing noise. I try again. Nothing.

Then I get it.

I press the little red button again and I say, "Reggie." I wait a second, and press the big black button.

"Reggie," the canister says in my voice.

Reggie looks up and cocks his head.

Awesome.

I reset all five canisters so that when you press the black buttons in order they say, "Nicky. And. Reggie. Were. Here." Hopefully, we'll be long gone before anyone figures it out. But it will be kind of cool when they do.

Suddenly I spy a phone on the wall. Why didn't I notice it before? It has gigantic buttons, and each of the numbers is also written in Braille dots. I go over and take the receiver off the hook to listen. The phone company hasn't shut it off yet!

From off my hand, I dial Rita's number.

"It's me, Nicky," I say when she picks up.

"Dude, where were you? I waited for you for, like, an hour."

"Sorry," I say. "Complications. Plus my mom called the police. They were swarming our apartment when we went by. They must be after Reggie."

"Are you sure they're not looking for *you*?" Rita says.

"The school principal went around to every class this afternoon asking whether anyone had seen you."

I explain the whole story about how Reggie misunderstood Mom's lame attempt at a high-five and tackled her, thinking he was protecting me. I tell her how freaked-out Mom was and how she made me lock him in the bathroom. I tell her I'm pretty sure Mom won't have Reggie back in the house for love nor money, but as far as I'm concerned, it has to be a package deal.

"Well, what are you going to do?" Rita says.

"Go live with my dad," I say. It just pops out of my mouth. But once it does, it makes total sense, because it'll kill two birds with one stone: save Reggie from the pound, and get me out of the mess I've made. Mom said he was working all weekend but I don't know that for sure. She lies. And so what if he is? Reggie and I can just hang out and play video games at his new place till he gets home from the office.

"Where does your dad live?" Rita says.

"I don't know," I admit. "An apartment somewhere in Littleton. Mom hasn't really let us see each other since we moved to Boston—even though he's supposed to get me two weekends a month. She keeps telling me he's busy."

"Why?"

"It's her way of getting back at him, I guess."

"You sure he's not just busy?" Rita says. "My mom would welcome a couple of weekends off from *me* every month. But, hey, it's your life. If you want, I can go online as soon as my mom gets off the computer and search the electronic White Pages in Littleton for your dad's address and phone number. What's his first name?"

I can't believe I never thought of that myself.

"Nicholas," I say. "Like mine: Nicholas Flynn."

"I'll call you right back," Rita says. "What's the number there?"

"I don't know," I say. "It's in Braille."

"Where the heck are you?" she says.

"It's a long story," I say. "I'll just call *you* in half an hour, OK?"

There's this big, long pause. "Nicky, I gotta tell ya, I really think you should try and work things out with your mom. I mean, she can't be all that bad, can she? There's got to be *some* reason you're living with her and not with your dad."

"Gotta go," I say. "I'll call you in thirty minutes."

"Don't do anything stupid," she says.

We hang up.

I stand there at the phone. For a second, I consider taking Rita's advice. I consider dialing our apartment on Eden Street. But in the end, I don't. In the end I dial the number of our old house back in Littleton. A recorded voice tells me the number has been disconnected, please hang up and dial again. I don't. I wait for the rapid beeping to stop. And into the dead silence I say, "Hello? Dad? It's me, Nicky.

Oh, I'm OK. Long time no see. I was walking the Freedom Trail today and thought of you. Hey, I finally got that dog I always wanted. He's a shepherd. His name is Reggie. Listen, Dad, I know you're a little busy this weekend. But Reggie and I are in kind of a tight spot. I was wondering if you could come into Boston and pick us up? We're over at Noyes Place in the North End. No, we're both OK. It's just a little misunderstanding. I'll explain everything when you get here."

I hang up. Role-playing is definitely overrated.

TWENTY MINUTES LATER. OLD ALF'S.

on't be fooled by old Westerns. Hiding out from the law is no fun. All you do is sit around wondering if you're going to get caught. There's still ten minutes to go before I can call Rita back. I'm sitting at the coffee table in the living room, losing at a game of Solitaire with Old Alf's deck of Braille cards. Reggie is snoring at my feet. I mean, literally. He sounds just like Mom when she dozes in front of the TV. But I don't poke Reggie with my toe to make him stop. He probably didn't get much shut-eye standing guard over me last night.

I can't stop thinking about Old Alf.

As anyone with cable TV knows, the evidence in a Dr. Ice case can sometimes suggest more than one possible outcome. I'm worried I may have jumped to a few too many conclusions. What if Alf Santorello is actually a nice enough old guy who is way into the latest gadgets. What if he's tried his best not to let his blindness get him down by leading a normal life, chatting and playing bocce with his old platoon buddies, buying cutlets at the local butcher shop. What if that's why he got Reggie in the first place—because a guide dog is way better than a cane for getting around. But what if Old Alf can't help but be a little cranky now and then, especially when cab drivers grab his arm—just like the duck boat driver did with me when I was pretending to be blind— or when nice neighbors like Jenny pet Reggie, even though he's clearly working. What if, with all he goes through each and every day, the intelligent disobedience clause of Reggie's contract just slipped Old Alf's mind. And what if, when he stepped out into the street with his mind on his troubles— even if Reggie tried to block the way—a bike messenger accidentally hit him?

"This is the place!" a loud voice outside says. "Just follow me!"

Reggie is up on his feet in a flash. He bounds over to the window to check out the situation.

"I'm not going to lie to you," says the voice. "She's been a little neglected lately. But underneath she has all her original charm."

I creep across the floor to peek through the blinds. It's dark out now, but from the orange glow of the streetlamps I can make out a man in a suit leaning against his car, talking to a young couple. He's bald and has nerdy glasses. He's carrying a clipboard in one hand, pointing with his pen at the house with the other. The three of them start walking toward the stoop.

"A real bargain for someone with a little vision and the handyman spirit."

"Time to make tracks!" I whisper to Reggie.

I scoop up the cards and stuff them into my knapsack. We both hightail it for the kitchen. I can hear them coming up the stoop. The real-estate guy tells the couple the place is being sold as is. If they don't want any of the furniture, arrangements can easily be made with Goodwill. That makes me feel a little better about taking the cards and compass and harness. Reggie and I slip out the back door just as the real-estate guy is opening the front one. We make a break for it down the little side alleyway as soon as they all step inside.

"Time for Plan D," I say to Reggie. "Or whichever one we're on now."

When we get to Prince Street, we don't turn toward Charlestown. Instead we cross it and keep heading up Salem. Before you know it, we're at the Old North Church, where Paul Revere saw the two lanterns the night of his midnight ride. The iron gate is locked up tight. Rats! But wait, I know for a fact there's a graveyard a little ways down Hull Street. It's called Copp's Hill Burying Ground. Dad and I shared a soda there the day we did the Freedom Trail.

I'm not so thrilled about the fact that I'm about to break into a misty old graveyard. But no one would ever find us there. And as soon as the gate is opened tomorrow, we could just sneak out. Unfortunately, all these thoughts of white patriot ghosts suddenly start popping into my head. I shove them aside as best I can. I'm too pooped, frankly, to find someplace less haunted.

I case the graveyard, just like on TV. The whole front side is fenced off. I don't remember if the fence runs all the way around or not. So I take Reggie down a side street called Snow Hill Avenue to find out. Near the end I spy a huge green construction dumpster leaning up against the fence. Whoever is fixing up their house across the street has parked their Cadillac beside the dumpster. "Come on, boy," I say, climbing up onto the hood. Reggie hesitates. "Forward!" I say in my best command voice. He whines, but obeys me and jumps up. The metal buckles a little under our weight and Reggie's toenails make a scratching sound that goes right through me. When I climb onto the Caddy's roof, though, Reggie follows me up the windshield without giving me a hard time. From there it's easy enough to hoist myself onto the top of the dumpster. Thank God it's closed!

I size up the iron fence. It has one of those spiky tops to keep out the riffraff. It's a little farther away from the dumpster than I thought, but I decide to jump over anyway. I command Reggie to sit, and I unhook his leash. I stuff it into my knapsack, then toss it into the graveyard. There's a loud glass-breaking sound when it hits the ground. Oops, forgot about the cereal bowl. Hope the talking compass is OK.

Sitting at the edge of the dumpster, I lower myself feet-first onto the top rail, placing my sneakers in between the spikes. I hold my breath and push off. For a second, I'm balanced on top of the fence, which feels really scary and kind of cool at the same time. Then I half jump, half fall into the graveyard. Well, mostly fall. I land pretty hard on my hands and knees. Luckily the grass is soft and wet. I scramble to my feet, wiping my hands on my pant legs.

Reggie whines from the top of the dumpster.

"Come on, boy," I say.

He looks down at me. He whines again.

"Come!" I say.

He crouches to jump. But he doesn't quite dare.

"Good boy," I say. "Really good boy."

He jumps then. He jumps clear over the fence. It's almost like he's flying for a few seconds—a phantom flying dog in the moonlight—and it's sort of beautiful to watch. He lands on his front paws first. But when his hind legs hit the ground, his right hip buckles beneath him. He squeals and struggles onto all fours. His bum leg! I totally forgot! It wobbles at first, but that doesn't stop ol' Reggie. He limps over to me and licks my hand.

I tell him to heel. I try rubbing his hind leg, like a massage, but he cries when I touch it. I look around for a place where we can rest. The pickings are pretty slim. So I lead him over to a long, flat tombstone the size of a human body—totally creepy, I know, but it's dry, at least. I stretch out on it, using my knapsack as a pillow. I pat the spot next to me. Reggie hobbles up, circles once or twice, and then settles onto his good hip with a groan. It's freezing out here, and I can see my breath. I wrap my arms around Reggie for warmth. "Sorry, boy," I whisper into his ear. "I didn't know what else to do."

I stroke the top of his head until he's asleep.

Rita. I forgot to call Rita.

I think about what she said on the phone. I'm sorry, but Mom has totally given me every excuse in the book why it never works out to spend a weekend with Dad. She always blames him. She's always saying Dad called or e-mailed or texted her at work to cancel, because he's under a lot of pressure at work, because he's got to take an unexpected business trip, because he's come down with the flu. Fact is, she *doesn't* want me to spend time with him. All because of the big mustard misunderstanding before the Fourth of July.

He *was* under a lot of pressure at work. He had a presentation to make for his boss—just like this weekend—so he could land some big promotion before we went away to Cape Cod. He really needed it. Mom liked to spend money. She was always buying something new for the house: some food processor for the kitchen or dwarf Japanese something-or-other for the garden. After a long day at the office, that twelve-dollar jar of mustard really set him off. That on top of the fact that I'd loaded a new video game onto his computer in the den without really knowing what I was doing, and I totally messed up his hard drive. Who could blame him? If only Mom could see Dad's side of the story, like I've been trying to see Old Alf's.

Except it still doesn't explain why Reggie freaks out whenever anyone raises their hand.

Better get some rest, Nicky.

I stare up at the stars. I try not to think about the ghosts of I-don't-know-how-many patriots waking up under the tombstones around us. I just keep counting to a thousand, waiting for morning to hurry up and get here.

PART THREE

IT'S A DOG-EAT-DOG WORLD

SATURDAY MORNING, EARLY. COPP'S HILL BURYING GROUND.

I wake up to some guy in a green uniform unlocking the front gate to the graveyard. He never even bothers to look over at the tombstones. He just climbs back into his green pickup, whistling, and drives away. It's a darn good thing. I'm so stiff from the cold, I doubt I could even run away. I rub my neck and check my watch. Just past seven o'clock. As usual, Reggie's standing guard beside me. I ask him how he's feeling. He sticks his pink tongue into my ear. So at least *he's* not mad at me right now.

I reach for my knapsack and dig out his last can of dog food. I open it up. My cereal bowl is busted into a million pieces, so I empty the food out onto the cement with my finger. Gross, I know, but it's an emergency. I chuck all the broken pieces of the bowl into the nearest trash can—no breakfast for me today—and wash my hands in a little fountain, making sure to scrub around Rita's number. Now that it's daylight, I see there's a pay phone over by the front gate. I put a quarter in and dial Rita's number. The call goes directly to her answering service: *¡Hola, es Rita! I'm either eating, sleeping, or in class, so leave a message at the beep. If this is Nicky, keep trying!*

I hang up and wander back to Reggie at the tombstone. I take a seat beside him and put my head in my hands to think. Now what?

If I can just get us to Littleton somehow, I'll call Rita for directions to Dad's from a phone booth. But how do I get us there? The commuter rail! Dad and I took the train to Boston the day we walked the Freedom Trail and saw the All-Star Wrestling Extravaganza. We caught it home from North Station, right next door to Boston Garden. North Station can't be too far from the North End, right? They're both north. Anyway, it better not be. Reggie's definitely limping this morning.

I count how much money I've got left. A little over three dollars. Three dollars and thirteen cents. I wonder if that's enough for a commuter rail ticket. I shove the money back into my pocket and put on my knapsack. "OK, Reggie," I say, hooking him to his leash. "I sure hope you're up for this." And I do. I really do.

We sneak out of the graveyard. Then I just keep asking everyone we run into where North Station is. At one point we pass through this gigantic open-air market, where all sorts of people are wandering around buying fresh vegetables and fruits.

I ask a guy who has a cartload of apples for directions. While he's pointing out where to go, I tuck an apple into each of my front pockets. I know—but it's an emergency!

When we finally get to North Station, I hitch Reggie's leash to the bicycle rack outside. I pat his head and tell him I'll be back in a jiff. He doesn't argue. He's more than ready for a rest. I head straight for the information booth. The lady behind the counter hands me a commuter rail schedule when I ask about trains to Littleton. I sit with Reggie and eat both apples while I figure it out. Supposedly there's a train every hour on the hour till eight o'clock. So that's good. I check the price table. It definitely looks cheaper if you're under twelve. That's really good. But a one-way ticket still costs way more than three dollars and thirteen cents. And it doesn't say anything about how much extra for pets.

I stand up. I untie Reggie's leash.

"Sorry, boy," I say. "Time for Plan Whatever."

We must actually be on Plan G or H by now. But I'm tired of keeping track.

SATURDAY MORNING. OUTSIDE NORTH STATION.

I stick out my thumb.

Cars whoosh by. A few of them honk—losers. No one

stops for us, though. I check the compass again. "North by northwest," it says. So this should be an OK street to take. Back in our old neighborhood, Mom was always telling people Littleton was a quiet little suburb northwest of Boston.

We wait. We wait. We wait some more. Hours go by, seems like, before anyone stops. Well, maybe not hours. But a really long time.

It's a young guy in an overnight delivery van.

"Dude, where you headed?" he says.

I tell him.

"That's like twenty-five miles away, man. I only make local deliveries," he says.

"Are you going past any roads that might take me there?" I say.

"Who knows?" he says. "You probably need Storrow Drive. But they change which streets you can use every freaking day around here. That's the Big Dig for you, man."

"Does that mean yes or no?" I say.

"Hop in," he says. "We'll soon see." He starts clearing parcels off the passenger seat. I roll the van's cargo door open for Reggie. The back is full of packages. I try not to look too relieved. But I feel a whole lot better knowing this guy has to *be* someplace soon.

I command Reggie to hop up inside.

His ears go flat. He sits down out on the tarmac.

"Forward!" I say.

He looks away from me.

I climb into the van myself and tug on his collar.

He lies down in the road.

"Ol' Rin Tin Tin's not into it, eh?" the driver says. He pulls a ziplock bag of dog biscuits out of the glove compartment. "Here, try one of these," he says, winking. "Deliveryman's best friend."

I try luring Reggie into the van with a biscuit. Nothing doing. I wave it in front of his nose. He *must* be hungry by now—I know *I* am—but he won't even sniff it. "It's not going to work," I tell the driver, "he won't go."

I climb out and shut the cargo door. I try handing the biscuit back, but the driver tells me to keep it, no problem, he's got plenty. I put it in my pocket and ask him how far away he thinks Storrow Drive is. He says not that far, just on the other side of the station and over by the substance abuse hospital. I don't bother to ask him why he didn't say so in the first place. I don't want to know. I just thank him and he drives off.

Reggie stumbles to his feet. He laps my hand. I dig the biscuit out of my pocket and give it to him. He eats it in two bites. I give him a good scratch behind the ears. What else are you going to do with eighty pounds of intelligently disobedient German shepherd?

"Looks like we're walking," I say.

As usual he sticks his tongue in my ear.

"Gross," I say. "Dog biscuit breath."

LATER SATURDAY MORNING. STORROW DRIVE.

Lucky for me, this part of the highway runs along the Esplanade, so there's someplace to walk—sort of. But it's true what Mom is always saying about Boston drivers. We've been dodging pickups and taxi cabs since we started. At least it's a really beautiful day out. Not a cloud in the sky. I've got my jacket wrapped around my middle. Indian summer. Supposedly it's based on the term "Indian giver": the gift of a few summer days in the fall that get taken back again by winter. The Native Americans supposedly gave all sorts of gifts to the Pilgrims—like their land—that were only symbolic. The Pilgrims didn't get that, and were really ticked off when the Native Americans wanted everything back after the first Thanksgiving, which caused the French and Indian War. Or something like that. Anyway, it's hot. And this knapsack sure is getting heavy. I have no idea how long it will take to get to Littleton. But I can't make Reggie go any faster. His hip is really acting up now. He's half limping, half hopping to avoid using his bum leg.

I stop for a second to dig those ugly black sunglasses out of my knapsack. A big-ass SUV comes screeching to a halt ahead of us. It idles beside the road, in spite of all the honking cars swerving around it, waiting for us to catch up. The people inside must think Reggie and I are still trying to hitch a ride. I wave them on, but they don't budge. When we eventually get to the SUV's passenger-side door, the window hums down.

It's Timmy Burns.

I blink once or twice to make sure it's not just sunstroke or something. No, it's really Timmy Burns.

"Hey," he says.

"Hey," I say back.

"My dad made us stop to see if you're OK," he says.

"Everything's fine," I say.

"OK," he says. "See you, then." The window starts to go up.

"Wait!" Mr. Burns shouts from the driver's seat. "What are you doing wandering down a busy highway like this all by yourself?"

Think quick, Nicky. "I'm on my way to the Hatch Shell," I say. "I usually run my dog out there. My mom couldn't drive me today. Her car's in the shop."

"No kidding! That's where we're going," Mr. Burns says. "Hop in!"

Timmy rolls his eyes at me. I can't tell whether it means *Don't you dare* or *Sorry my dad's being such a loser.*

"Thanks anyway," I say. "But my dog is kind of funny about getting into strange vehicles."

"You sure?" Mr. Burns says. "It's pretty far."

"May as well give it a try," Timmy says, real cool-like. He reaches around and opens the back passenger-side door.

I hesitate. He has, after all, been trying to beat me up for a solid week. But they have water fountains at the Esplanade, and Reggie and I could sure use a drink. There's also that hot dog cart, and I still have three dollars and thirteen cents. So I climb up onto the backseat. I say, "Come on, Reggie." I don't put my heart into it, though. It's not even a real command. He cocks his head and whines. "See what I mean?" I say. "He won't do it. He was trained to be my guard dog as a puppy."

"Yeah, you said," Timmy says. "Try again."

"Come, Reggie," I say. He hesitates. He puts his forepaw up onto the running board. He takes it back down.

"It's no use," I say, relieved.

"Come on fella," Timmy says. "It's OK."

Reggie whines, then struggles up onto the seat beside me, dragging his bum leg behind. I reach over to help him the rest of the way. He yelps, but soon he's settled onto his good side and I've shut the door behind him. I strap on my seat belt. "I guess we're ready to roll," I say, feeling totally trapped. Mr. Burns peels back onto the road in a spray of gravel behind us.

No one says much at first, which is fine by me. Then Mr. Burns says, "It was Timmy here who spotted you."

"Tim, not Timmy," Timmy says.

Whatever.

"Timmy said you two were school chums," Mr. Burns says.

"I did not!" Tim says. He turns to face me and rolls his eyes again. "What I said was, 'That looks like the new kid from homeroom who dumped that bag of dog food all over the Supa-Sava.'"

I don't say anything. I don't really want to get into it. I've got bigger problems to worry about than how much this kid hates my guts.

"Nicky, right?" he says.

"Yeah," I say. So he does know my actual name.

"I'm Tim," he says. "Not Timmy."

"Yeah," I say. "I know."

"What's your dog's name again?"

"Reggie," I say.

"Reggie?" he says.

"Don't look at me," I say, "I didn't name him. He came that way."

"Reggie's an all-right name," Tim says. "Reggie's cool. Aren'tcha, boy?" He reaches over and pats Reggie's head.

Reggie licks his hand. Traitor. I shoot him a dirty look. He won't get into a delivery van for love nor money, but he's got no problem hanging out with, like, my biggest enemy in the entire universe.

Tim starts fiddling with the radio. He picks a hip-hop station. It's way better than the heavy metal Mom likes. We don't talk for the rest of the drive over to the Hatch Shell. It doesn't feel weird, though. It actually feels OK.

"Everybody out," Mr. Burns says when we find a parking space. He and Tim start unpacking the SUV. They've got a couple of lawn chairs back there, a big nylon bag, and some extra jackets and stuff. I wait till they're not really looking and then I help Reggie down. I don't want him jumping on that leg anymore. We've still got a long ways to go. I lead him over to a fountain for joggers. I make a cup of water with my hands. Reggie laps up ten straight handfuls.

Mr. Burns and Tim are staring at us.

"Well, thanks again for the lift," I say.

Mr. Burns holds up the nylon bag. "We're going over to the island to fly the kite I got Timmy for his birthday," he says. "Want to tag along?"

"I probably need to rest Reggie first," I say. "His hip has gotten a little stiff from dodging traffic."

"I noticed he was limping pretty bad," Tim says. "That's how I recognized it was you."

He's not limping all *that* bad.

Yes he is, Nicky. He totally is.

"You sure you don't want to come along?" Mr. Burns says. "It's one of those trick kites."

"Another time, maybe," I say.

"Suit yourself," Mr. Burns says, gathering up the lawn chairs. "Let's go, Timmy—before all the good spots get taken."

"I'll be right there," Tim says.

"Don't forget your jacket," Mr. Burns says. "It's windy out there."

"Obviously," Tim whispers, under his breath.

The two of us watch Mr. Burns head across the Hatch

Shell lawn to the island where the kite-flyers are. As soon as his father's out of earshot, Tim turns to me and says, "You weren't in school yesterday. Everyone was going mental. The principal asked in every class if anybody had seen you. You running away or something?"

"Yeah," I say.

"Wow," he says. "What did you do?"

For some reason, I tell him. I tell him everything. I don't know why. Maybe because my dogs are tired after being on the lam for so long. Maybe because I didn't get much sleep last night—or the night before. Or because I haven't been able to reach Rita yet today. And because I really miss Marky right now and I would have told Marky everything. But I tell Tim all about Reggie being an ex-seeing-eye-career-change-dog, not a guard dog. I tell him how Reggie's ex-master, Old Alf, fired him for unknown reasons, which landed Reggie in the pound. I tell him how Reggie led me around Boston as if I was blind and introduced me to all sorts of people, like Sal and the old guys, Mrs. Strazzulo, and Jenny. How I let everyone believe I was Old Alf's grandson, until the mail-man sort of caught me. How Reggie went mental on Mom because he thought she was trying to attack me when she was only high-fiving. I explain about taking off in the middle of the night after Mom threatened to send Reggie back to the pound. About doing the Freedom Trail and sneaking onto a duck boat. About breaking into Old Alf's empty house and sleeping there. I tell him how we nearly got caught by the real-estate guy, how Reggie hurt his hip sneaking into the graveyard, how we didn't have enough money to buy a train ticket back to Littleton in the suburbs. How we decided to hitchhike there instead.

"Littleton? Why are you going *there*?" Tim says.

"It's where my dad lives," I say. I hope.

"Your parents split up too?" Tim says.

"Yeah," I say. "They're getting a divorce. They're just waiting for the papers to go through." And it's weird. It's the very first time I've ever actually said that word—*divorce*—out loud to anyone before. Not to Rita, not even to Dr. Holkke.

"Wow," Tim says. "You're, like, *crazy*."

"I go to a shrink every Wednesday," I admit.

"Doesn't it suck?" he says. "I go Thursdays after school."

"Big-time," I agree.

"So now what are you going to do?" he says.

"Keep hitchhiking, I guess."

"I wouldn't," Tim says.

"Why not?"

"Are you kidding? Every cop in Chucktown is probably on the lookout for a kid with a shepherd. There's probably a citywide APB out on you right now. You know how grown-ups get about missing children. You're a sitting duck. Especially the way Reggie's limping."

"You think so?" I say.

"Trust me," he says. "You're better off taking the train."

Even though he's still technically my archenemy, I know

he's right. Plus I shouldn't really be making Reggie walk on that hind leg. Even Tim can see that, and he's below grade level in both math and English.

"Do you have any money on you?" I say. "I'll pay you back."

He shakes his head no. "How much you need again?" he says.

I tell him.

"I've got an idea," he says. "If you come and pretend to fly kites with us for a while, my dad'll probably offer to buy us hot dogs and stuff for lunch. The two of us will volunteer to go and get food at the cart, but we'll only buy a couple of franks for Dad and pretend we already ate ours. You can pocket all the rest of the money."

"Won't he ask for the change?" I say. Actually, a hot dog sounds pretty good to me right now. I didn't have any breakfast, except for the apples.

"He won't even notice. He's way into this kite thing. It's kind of embarrassing."

"You think it'll work?" I say.

"Trust me," he says. "On the way back to Chucktown, you can have him drop you off at North Station."

"OK," I say.

"But if you tell anybody about the kite flying, I'll beat you to a pulp."

"I won't be going back to Chucktown," I say.

It's a pretty good plan, I have to admit. I'm dying to ask

him why he's being so nice to me all of a sudden. But I don't press my luck. Instead I hook Reggie to his leash and begin walking over to the kite-flying island.

"Mind if I hold him?" Tim says.

I do. I really do. But I hand him Reggie's leash.

Tim is right. Mr. Burns is way into the kite-flying thing. He can make Tim's kite dodge and dip wherever he wants it to go. Tim and I both suck. We can usually get the kite up, but the minute we try to do any real tricks, it makes a nosedive for the ground. Then Mr. Burns says, *No, no, not like that!* and takes it back to show us. We don't get to fly it again for ages. We don't really care, though. We're only pretending to have fun.

Meanwhile Reggie just lies there, under a bench, panting. I don't think I've ever seen him look so pooped out. That's it. We're definitely taking the train.

After a while, Tim says, "Hey Dad, I'm getting hungry. Can you buy me and Nicky something to eat?"

"Sure," Mr. Burns says. "How about hot dogs?"

Tim winks at me. "Sounds great," he says.

Mr. Burns takes a twenty out of his wallet.

"It's probably going to be a little more than that," Tim says. "There's three of us, don't forget."

Mr. Burns takes out another ten, shaking his head.

"Let's go," Tim says to me.

"OK," I say, trying not to laugh.

"Come on, Reggie," Tim says.

Reggie's ears perk up, but he doesn't budge. He looks to me for a command.

"Forward," I say. Reggie struggles to his feet, but he hobbles right over to lick my hand. Attaboy! They say every dog has his day, and this one is Reggie's. He's not giving up the fight, even though he's been wounded in action. He's an honest-to-God trouper, which is what *I* would have named him if I'd been given the chance. And no kid ever had a more loyal sidekick.

The three of us head over to the snack cart. Reggie needs to take his time, and Tim and I let him, since we're talking anyway about what a goofball Gilmore can be.

At the snack cart, we do a bunch of math and figure out that we can actually buy two hot dogs and a soda for Tim's dad, plus one hot dog each for us, plus a large fries to split and still have enough for a train ticket for me, plus a dollar and change extra for emergencies—as long as we both skip sodas and take long drinks at the water fountain instead. We order the food, and while we're waiting, we check out the stand that sells kites and Frisbees. I don't tell Tim about the Superman kite Mom and I got. Instead I tell him I've been meaning to teach Reggie how to fetch a Frisbee but haven't had the chance yet, what with his bum leg. Tim says dogs that catch Frisbees are awesome.

When the food's ready, we bring it over to a picnic table. I take a really big bite of hot dog. Out of the corner of my eye, I see Reggie giving me a *What about me?* look.

Suddenly I feel terrible. I was so hungry, I didn't even think. I immediately divide what's left of my hot dog in half and give him the slightly bigger piece. He wolfs it in a couple of bites. I pop the rest into my own mouth.

"What did you do that for?" Tim says. "I would have eaten the rest, if you're not hungry."

"I'm starving," I say. "But Reggie and I are in this together. It's fifty-fifty, all the way—right, boy?" I pat his head.

Reggie licks my hand.

Tim doesn't say anything, but I can tell he's jealous.

"We'd better bring your dad his food," I say. "Before it's totally cold."

"Yeah, I guess so," Tim says.

When we get to the stone bridge, though, Tim tells me to stop. He says he'll be right back. He makes me hold his dad's food box and runs over to the snack cart. A few minutes later, he comes running back with another hot dog and hands it to me. "Here," he says. "Split it with Reggie."

"Where did you get the money?" I say. As far as I know, I have all the rest of the change.

He grins. "I told the guy behind the counter you dropped your hot dog and Reggie snarfed it up on you," he says. "I said you were too embarrassed to ask for another one yourself."

"Not bad," I say.

"You're not the only smart kid in that stupid school," he says.

About an hour later, Tim complains he's bored. Mr. Burns asks him if he wants to go bowling instead. Tim rolls his eyes at me and says, *Yeah, whatever.* We pack everything up and head for the SUV. Once we're on the road, Mr. Burns asks me if I want to come along. I tell him no, my mom's picking me up at North Station in a little while.

"I thought you said her car was on the blink?" he says.

Oops. "The garage she uses is right around the corner from there," I say. "They promised to have it ready by this afternoon. We've got errands to run."

"Back in Chucktown," Tim says, changing the radio station.

"Yeah, back in Chucktown," I say.

"Oh," Mr. Burns says. "Another time, then."

"Yeah, another time," I say.

At the station, I thank Mr. Burns for the ride and the hot dogs and stuff. Tim turns around and gives Reggie a final pat on the head. Reggie licks his hand. He seems to have perked up a little, thank God, with some food in his belly.

"See you in school on Monday," Tim says, winking again.

"See you Monday," I say.

I help Reggie out of the car. Mr. Burns waves good-bye and peels out of the station, laying a big patch of rubber.

Why do grown-ups think kids like to go bowling?

■■■

SATURDAY AFTERNOON.
NORTH STATION.

There's a conductor straight ahead, at the entrance to the platforms. He's watching everybody pass through the gate. I pull Reggie's work harness out of my knapsack and strap it on him. I put my big black sunglasses back on. I whisper, "You know the drill," and command Reggie forward. Together we walk right past the conductor like we own the place.

"Hang on a minute," he says.

"Stop!" I command Reggie. I turn in the conductor's direction. "Yes?"

"Ticket please," the conductor says.

I hand him the ticket I just bought with Tim's dad's money.

"That your guide dog?" he says.

Obviously.

"We need platform six," I say.

"Here, I'll help you over there," he says. Before he can grab my arm, though, I say, "I would really prefer if you didn't touch me, not unless I ask."

"Oh," the conductor says. "What should I do?"

"Show my dog where you'd like us to go. It's his job to lead me."

"OK," the conductor says. "Come on, boy, this way."

Reggie draws himself up to full attention. He puffs out his chest. He glances back, waiting for my command. Do I dare? Do I let him prove to me, once and for all, that he really is good at his job?

I close my eyes really tight.

Guide me, I think. "Forward!" I say.

Gently, ever so gently, Reggie leads me in the direction of the conductor's voice.

The conductor's heels slap against cement as he walks away. People rush past, trying to make their connections— their worry like wind on my face. Reggie strains against his harness to pull me forward. The harness leather creaks as the handle jerks and sways in my hand because Reggie's limping. He has a raspy edge to his breath that I don't like. The conductor calls from somewhere ahead: *Here, boy, over here.* The train ticks and hums, getting louder and louder. The shadow of an enormous train falls, somehow, across my face. Dry heat and exhaust. Stench of oil and soot.

"You're almost there," the conductor says, from above. "You've got a couple of steep steps now."

I don't open my eyes. Reggie tenses at the end of the harness. He's not sure he can make the steps. He waits for my command. "Forward," I say. "Please, boy, for me."

Reggie jumps up onto the first step and groans. I'm desperate to open my eyes, but I don't. Because if he can make it, I can too. If he doesn't get to cheat, why should I? We're in this together. Fifty-fifty. I put out my hand. The hot side of the train. Dirty and hot, smelling of soot. I grope for the rail. I raise my foot—to where? It feels like I'm jumping off a cliff—but my sneaker lands solidly on the first step. Reggie staggers up to the second. Together we make our way, step by step, up into the front of the car.

"You OK?" the conductor says.

I nod, trying to catch my breath. But I don't open my eyes.

"Can you take it from here?" he says. "The train's about to pull out of the station."

I nod. But I'm not so sure. He steps off. When the car lurches forward a second later, I almost lose my balance. That throws me into a complete panic. I should have asked him how far away the seats are. I should just open my eyes now. Why don't I just open my eyes and see where I am?

No. Not yet.

"Aisle or window?" a man says not too far away. "There's an empty window seat right here beside me in the front row, but I'm not fussy."

"Window's fine," I say.

"Here, boy," the man says.

Reggie leads me over to the empty seat. I slump into it. It feels like the best thing in the entire world. Because we made it. Because Reggie got me here safely. Because he did his job perfectly. He positions himself between my legs and

I give him a congratulations pat. He hunkers down to the floor with a little groan.

"Your dog doesn't look so good," the man says, beside me.

"His hip bothers him sometimes," I say, trying not to freak out. "I'm taking him straight to the vet as soon as I get home."

"Want me to put your knapsack up in the rack?" he says. "It'll give you both more room."

I don't, actually. I just want to sit here and hug it. But I hand it over, mostly because I don't want Reggie to see how worried I am.

The man stows my bag and sits back down. I can hear him turning the pages of a newspaper. I can actually smell the ink. I'm dying to sneak a better look at him, but I still refuse to open my eyes. By his voice, I'm guessing he's about my dad's age, maybe a little younger. I wonder if he's handsome like my dad, if he has the same color hair and eyes, if he's wearing a suit.

The train starts to pick up speed.

"Thanks," I say. "For not grabbing me, I mean. It freaks me out—the thought of people grabbing at me when I can't see them."

"No problem," he says. "My nephew's blind. I hear all the horror stories."

All the horror stories. I can't even imagine what it would be like—to have people grabbing at you and pulling you after them all day, yelling at you when your hearing is probably

twice as good as theirs, talking about you like you aren't
standing right in front of them. Seriously, what if you had
to go through what I just went through all the time?—ten
times a day, maybe? It wouldn't be your own blindness that
was a drag. It would be the blindness of everyone around
you. I swear, as soon as I decide to open my eyes, I will
never, *ever* pull this little blind-man's-bluff again.

I think of Alf Santorello.

Truth is, I'll probably never know what actually happened
between him and Reggie. I'm off the case. Some other kid'll
have to sift through all the evidence and decide. And even
if I did know what caused Old Alf to fire Reggie, I'll never
know what life was like for him as a blind taxi dispatcher
before that, or a disabled veteran of the Korean War before
that. I'm not blind. I'm only faking it for a train ride. Maybe
I shouldn't have yelled at Old Alf up at Monument Square.
But I'm sticking to what I said. Because no matter how
frustrated he may have gotten with the world, it would still
have been wrong to take his anger out on Reggie. Even if
raising his cane was only a threat. End of story.

"That was a heavy sigh," the man says.

"It's been kind of a long day," I say.

"Tell me about it," he says. "I hate working Saturdays."

"Can I ask you a question?" I say.

"Shoot."

"What do you think about bowling?"

"Stupid sport," he says. "Ridiculous shoes."

"Can I ask you another question?"

"Go for it."

"Are you married?"

"No."

"Divorced?"

"No," he says. "You?"

I laugh and shake my head. "The kids at school make fun of me because they think I have this girlfriend named Rita," I say. "But she's not my *girl*friend, just a friend. She was the first person to be nice to me at my new school. Everybody else gave me a pretty hard time."

"Kids are rotten," the man says.

"So you don't want kids?" I say.

"No."

"Too bad," I say.

"Why's that?" he says.

"I don't know," I say. "Seems like you'd make a decent dad."

"I doubt it," he says. "Good parents always put their kids' needs before their own. I don't think I could do that yet. I'm kind of selfish. Right now I'm more interested in building my career, riding my motorcycle, having a few laughs with my friends."

"Oh," I say. "Thanks."

"For what?" he says.

"For telling me the truth."

"No problem," he says.

The train makes its first two stops. People get off.

People get on. The next time the train slows, though, the man stands up. He fetches his briefcase from the overhead rack and shoves his newspaper into it. Then he takes my knapsack down and sets it into his empty seat for me.

"This your stop?" I say. Obviously.

"Yup."

"Have a good weekend," I say.

"You too," he says, setting off down the aisle.

That's when I finally open my eyes. I lift the sunglasses up, so I can look out the window and watch a man who looks nothing like my dad stroll across the platform swinging his briefcase as he heads toward the parking lot. The train starts to move again. We round a corner. The man disappears.

I check on Reggie. He's totally passed out at my feet, poor thing. The corners of his mouth are all gummy with white spit. But at least he's breathing a little easier now. I'm dying to scratch him behind the ears the way he likes, tell him how sorry I am for dragging him into this mess. Later. I don't want to wake him. He's going to need all the strength he can muster for whatever's next.

I put the sunglasses back on, just in case a conductor comes by. We've got at least a half-dozen more stops before Littleton. I fish around in my knapsack for the Braille cards. I run my fingers over the bumps of each one, trying to figure out which bumps are numbers and which mean spades, clubs, diamonds, and hearts.

LATE SATURDAY AFTERNOON. LITTLETON STATION.

There's a pay phone in the waiting room. I plunk one of my last quarters into the slot. Rita picks up on practically the first ring. "Nicky is that you?" she says.

"I tried calling earlier, but your machine picked up. Things got a little crazy after that."

"Where are you?" she says.

"At the train station in Littleton," I say. "Did you find my dad's address?"

"There were a gazillion Flynns out there," she says. "But only one had the first initial *N*. The address is 22 Resolution Road, Unit D. Do you want me to log back on to the Internet, call up a map of Littleton, and GPS you over there?"

"No, I know where Resolution Road is," I say. "It's only a couple of blocks from my old house on King Street. In fact, I have to walk right past it."

"You want his phone number?"

I tell her yes. She gives it to me. I repeat it three times until it's burned into my memory.

"Call me as soon as you know what's what," Rita says.

"OK," I say.

Then I hang up. There's plenty left on the quarter. I've just run out of words.

▭▭▭

TWENTY MINUTES LATER.
MY OLD HOUSE.

The For Sale sign is still stuck into the front lawn. The mailbox still has our last name on it. Reggie and I stand under the maple where Marky and I were building our tree fort this past summer. I point out the house. "That's where I used to live," I tell Reggie. "Isn't it nice?" Reggie doesn't seem all that interested. He just sits and pants. Well, it's more like wheezing now, and he's all foamy at the mouth. Plus he can't really put any weight on his hind leg. I guess I didn't realize just how long the walk would take from the station—I only ever rode the commuter train that once with Dad, and we drove down there in his BMW.

Actually, the old place isn't looking its best. One of the shutters of a living room window is hanging at a crazy angle. The paint on the garage door is peeling. The grass hasn't been mowed in ages, and no one has been looking after Mom's flower beds—her asters and mums have all dried up and turned the same color brown. Still, this place beats anything in Chucktown by, like, a mile and a half.

I show Reggie which window was my old bedroom on the second floor. I point out Marky's house, a couple of driveways down. I describe where the in-ground swimming pool was supposed to go.

I run out of things to say after that.

"Mom had to put it on the market," I tell Reggie. "She

told me over and over again it was because she wanted a new beginning—a fresh new start—but I know that's not the real reason. I heard her talking on the phone with her friends. The real reason is, she couldn't afford to pay all the monthly bills on a house this size, even though Dad was willing to give her the place in the settlement. There's no way Mom could ever find the same kind of decent-paying job Dad has. She hasn't worked since college. That's why she only answers the phone and types for the Ambulance Chasers. That's why we live in the dump we live in now."

I stick my hand out. Reggie doesn't nuzzle it. It seems to be way too much effort for him. "Come on, boy," I say. "Forward, I mean. Just a little farther, I promise."

He doesn't budge. He's not being intelligently disobedient. It's obvious he wants to go with me, but can't. He can't go another step.

Oh crap! Crap, crap, crap!

Hold it together, Nicky. Just a little while longer, until you find your dad. You're Reggie's master now. He's counting on you.

Gently, I coax Reggie to lie down. I unstrap his harness and shove it up into the half-built fort. I cover him with my coat and tuck it in. I tell him to stay. As if! There's no way he's going to wander off, not in his condition.

I half walk, half run to Resolution Road. And it's weird. Because I notice things about the neighborhood I never noticed before. All the streets are lined with gigantic old trees, for instance. And everybody has at least one super-nice car in the driveway—usually two. All the names on the mailboxes are like Burns and Ross, Johnson and Jackson, not like Singh or Rubenstein or Wong, which are the names of some of the kids in my class. Or de la Cruz.

I walk right past Marky's house. I'm so tempted to stroll up to the front door and ring the bell. Marky's got bunk beds. Plus they had a dog once, so I know for a fact there's a spare doghouse out back. Marky's dad would know exactly what to do about Reggie. He's in the army.

But that's not who I'm here to see. I'm here to see Dad.

Turns out, 22 Resolution Road isn't a house. It's a whole gated community—about a dozen two-story condos all built to *look* like brick town houses, weirdly enough. They're brand-new with nice, little front porches and upstairs balconies and shutters on the windows. Plus they form a big *U* around a built-in pool. It looks more like a little fishing village on Cape Cod than any street in Boston, if you ask me—not that I've ever been there.

I don't even need to hunt for Unit D. My dad's black Beamer is parked outside the condo two doors down on the left. It's gleaming in the setting sunlight. So at least he's not working too late tonight. I shiver a little. I could really use my coat about now. But Reggie needed it more.

I head for the front porch. I take a deep breath and knock on the door. I see from my own reflection in the storm window that I'm still wearing those stupid sunglasses. I whip them off and stuff them into the sumac on my right. Sumac. Another one of those S-and-a-vowel words.

Just in the nick of time. Because suddenly I'm not staring at myself through the glass anymore. I'm looking right at my dad. He's not in a suit. He's in a polo shirt and chinos. His salesman smile vanishes the second he recognizes me.

"What are you doing here?" he says.

"Hi, Dad," I say.

"Where's your mother?" he says, peering over my shoulder for her car in the driveway. Not: *Oh my God, it's Nicky!* Not: *I haven't seen you in ages!* Not: *I've thought about you a million times, buddy!*

"It's just me," I say. "Can I, um, come in?"

Dad blinks a couple of times, like I've just asked him in Swedish. "Yeah, sure, buddy, of course," he says.

I step past him into his living room, which is actually one big gigantic ground-floor room that has a kitchen and dining room and living room all in one. It's nice—too nice—with everything matchy-matchy, which, if you've ever looked for an apartment yourself, is how you can tell it came already furnished.

"Seriously, Nick," Dad says, checking his watch. "What *are* you doing here?"

"I've decided to stay with you for a while," I say. "Isn't that great?"

"You can't!" he says. "I mean, that's not what the judge decided when your mother and I separated."

"He said you have the right to see me on a regular basis."

"Sure, a couple of weekends a month," Dad says. "But not to live here. I'm not even set up for that. Look how tiny this place is."

I look around. It's much bigger than the apartment on Eden Street. Plus this couch would be way nicer to sleep on. Plus there's an upstairs I haven't even seen yet.

"Wait, does your mother even know you're here?" Dad says.

"Mom's a big fat liar," I say. "She's always telling me you've canceled our weekends together because something last-minute came up. She said you were working on a presentation all weekend. It's obvious she just doesn't want me to see you."

Dad checks his watch again. He runs his hand through his hair. "Sit down," he says. "Let's both sit down."

I take a seat on the couch. He sits in the armchair opposite. "I got another promotion recently," he says. "They've made me the big boss now, sales director of all Massachusetts. I've got tons more responsibility. A lot of people are counting on me. When I do get a day or two off, I really need to relax."

"So you're not working this weekend," I say.

"I told your mom I'd definitely set something up for next weekend," Dad says. "It's on my list. Didn't she tell you?"

On his list to build a swimming pool in the backyard. On his list to help me and Marky finish the tree fort. On his list to take us all to the Cape on the Fourth of July for vacation. On his list to teach me how to throw a Frisbee.

Mom wasn't lying to me after all. He's been canceling every one of our upcoming weekends together. How could I be so blind?

Not now, Nicky. This needs to be about Reggie right now, not you.

"Listen, Dad," I say. "I really need your help. Things are a little tense between me and Mom at the moment. We have this new dog now, Reggie, and there's been a little misunderstanding—"

"What new dog?" Dad says. "She let you have a dog?"

"Yeah, his name is Reggie. He's a purebred shepherd. But listen—"

"Figures! I've wanted to get you a dog for years," he says. "Your mother always shot me down. Too messy, too much work. Now suddenly she's the hero. Well, getting a dog was *my* idea, not hers—"

"Listen," I say. "Reggie's had an accident and I *really* need your help—"

The front doorbell rings. We both jump about a foot.

Dad puts his head in his hands. He sighs. "Come on in," he says. "It's open."

A lady walks through the front door. She's carrying a bag of groceries. She's pretty. A real babe.

"That's Lori," Dad says. "Lori, meet my son, Nicholas."

Lori's all smiles. She comes right over and shakes my hand. "Your dad's told me so much about you," she says. "What a nice surprise! Are you staying for dinner? I'm making pork chops. I bought extra."

Suddenly I'm back in our old kitchen, pretending to read a Dr. Ice comic book at the table. Dad's yelling at Mom for buying a twelve-dollar jar of mustard. He's telling her she needs to learn a little self-control. She turns away from the pork chops sizzling on the stove. That's rich, she says, coming from him. What's his new secretary's name again— Lonnie? Loren? He tells her to stop being so paranoid. She tells him to stop giving her reasons to be. It's the wine talking now, he says. Go to hell, she says.

"Nicky and I are just having a little chat," Dad tells Lori, before I can answer one way or the other about dinner. "Then we're calling his mother so she can come and get him."

"Oh. OK," Lori says. "Some other time, then." She heads for the kitchen counter and starts unpacking groceries.

"What were you saying about a dog?" Dad says, remembering, finally, that I'm, like, another human being on the planet.

"Nothing," I say. "I'd better get going." I stand to leave.

"Where?" he says. "Back to Charlestown? On your own?"

"Mom's meeting me over at the old house," I say.

"What's she doing over there?" Dad says.

"Can I use your bathroom real quick?" I say.

"First door on the right down that hallway," Lori says, pointing.

I lock myself in the john. I feel kind of dizzy all of a sudden. I run cold water in the sink so I can splash my face with it. But I don't. Instead I race over to the toilet and fling up the lid—just in time. I puke up every last bit of the hot dog I had for lunch.

IT ALL COMES FLOODING BACK . . .

Dad grabs Mom by the arm. He yanks her around to face him. He holds the twelve-dollar jar of mustard an inch away from her face. This has got to stop, he says. Do you hear?

—Take your hands off me, she says. Now!

—No, you're going to listen to me for a change, Dad says.

I jump up from where I'm supposedly reading a comic book.

—Stop it, both of you! I yell. I can't take it anymore! Who cares how much a jar of mustard costs?

—And *you*, Dad says, turning to me. You stay out of this. You're still not out of the doghouse with me for frigging up my computer.

—You *told* me to load that new video game onto it, I say.

—I didn't tell you to wipe out the hard drive! he says.

—I asked you to show me how, I say. You said you were too busy.

—Working my ass off to pay for twelve-dollar jars of mustard! he says. The pair of you! You're killing me!

He flings the jar of mustard against the wall. It bursts into a million pieces. Shards of glass tinkle to the floor tiles, leaving behind a big, yellow dripping sun. We all stare at it, speechless. The pork chops sizzle away in their skillet.

Mom yanks herself free of Dad's grip. She comes racing over and throws her arms around me.

—Take a walk around the block, she says to Dad. Cool yourself off.

—I will not, Dad says. You're both going to listen for a change.

—What's next? Mom says. Me against that wall? Your son? You've got to find a way to control your temper, Nick. I will not continue to put up with these violent outbursts! If you don't go and walk out your anger right now, I swear I'll call the cops.

—You will do no such thing, he says, stepping toward us. This is my house.

Mom backs us over to the wall phone. She picks up the receiver.

I wrench myself free and run upstairs. I lock myself in my room.

━ ━ ━

A FEW MINUTES LATER.
RESOLUTION ROAD.

Y ou OK?" Dad calls from the other side of the bathroom door.

"Fine," I say, flushing. "I'll be right out."

"You aren't being sick in there, are you?" he says.

"Just a bad cough," I say. "I can't seem to shake this cold."

"Oh, OK. Just checking."

I rinse my mouth out under the tap. Now I splash water on my face. I stare at myself in the mirror. Everybody says I look just like my dad. The very spit and image, they say. Nick off the old block.

It's true what Mickey said: The apple didn't fall very far from the tree. I've got quite a little temper on me too. But I swear I'm going to learn how to control *mine*. Because regretting that you've busted up a perfectly good Frisbee or written all over a fridge or flung crayons across the room *after* you've done it is way too late.

I wipe my palms on the back of my jeans. I run my hand through my wild mop. Mom's right. I *do* need a haircut. Bad.

I head back to the main room, where Dad is whispering something to Lori.

"I'd better be hitting the road," I say.

"Tell your mother I'll call her this week to set up a weekend with you," Dad says.

"Okeydokey," I say.

"Maybe the three of us can do something fun together in the city," Lori pipes up. "It's been ages since I've been to Boston."

"Sure," I say. "We'll go bowling."

Dad raises his hand. I jump back—then realize, too late, he's only trying to high-five me. I don't high-five him back. I just stick my hand out for a shake. He shakes, then gives me the sort of slap-on-the-back hug football players on TV always do after a touchdown. I head for the door.

Oh, he'll intend to call next week. But then something'll come up at work. He's totally into his career at the moment. Waxing his BMW on Saturday afternoons. Dating his secretaries. He's really not such a bad guy, my dad—not as bad, anyway, as Mom makes him out to be to her friends on the phone. In fact, you'd probably like him if you met him on the train. He just totally sucks at being a parent. For one thing, he doesn't handle stress very well. For another, he never follows through with a promise. And P.S., he has no clue how to put the needs of anyone else ahead of his own.

Reggie! I've got to get back to Reggie.

I tell Lori it was nice meeting her. Not! I say good-bye to Dad. And finally I'm out of there. I don't bother fishing those dollar sunglasses out of the sumac. The sun disappeared behind the trees ages ago. Anyway, I won't ever be needing them again.

◗◗◗

DUSK. LITTLETON TRAIN STATION.

I'm out of breath by the time I'm back at the waiting-room phone booth.

I lift up the receiver. *Please,* I say to myself, *please let just one thing go right today. Please.* I hear a tone, and dial zero. I give the operator the number and my name. Mom picks up on the second ring. The operator cuts in and asks if she'll accept charges from Nicky.

"Of course!" Mom says.

"It's me," I say. Obviously.

"Are you OK?" she says.

"Reggie's hurt," I say. "He needs to go to the animal hospital right away. Can you come and get us?"

"Where?" she says.

I tell her to meet us at our old house in Littleton. I tell her we'll be sitting under the tree fort.

"Oh God," she says. "I'll be right there. Don't move."

"I won't," I say.

"Promise me!" she says.

"I promise."

"I'll be right there," she says again, and hangs up.

I hang up. And I run. I run as fast as I can back to Reggie.

He's still at the tree fort, shivering under my coat. I sit cross-legged and lay his head in my lap. Reggie's eyes open. He looks up at me. And there's that big cartoon question mark floating between his ears.

"I messed up," I tell him. "I should never have made you jump off that dumpster. I knew about your hip. I knew that wouldn't be good for it. I've been a rotten master. And I totally deserve to have you taken away from me."

Reggie closes his eyes. The question mark fades away.

Now, at least, we both know the truth.

AFTER DARK. MY OLD HOUSE.

Mom's car comes squealing up the driveway. She jumps out and runs toward the tree fort without even shutting off the engine or closing the door. She skids to a halt when she sees us. "Oh my God!" she says.

"We need to get him straight to the vet," I say. I'm so tired it comes out like a whisper. "I'm afraid he's going to die."

"What happened? Are *you* OK?"

"Just help me get him into the car," I say. "I'll explain everything later. You can totally yell at me then—for as long as you like. But right now I really need your help."

"Nicky!"

"Please," I say. "Please, Mom."

She opens her mouth, but then closes it. Instead she crouches next to me. "OK," she says. "Just tell me what to do."

And I do. I tell her to drive the car over here to the tree. Across the lawn? she says. I nod. She doesn't even bother to say *But what about the grass?* While she's backing the car over, I whisper into Reggie's ear: "It's OK now, Mom's here." I say whatever comes to mind after that, to keep us both calm. "Oh, she's not perfect," I say. "She buys stupid things to make herself feel better. She listens to heavy metal and forgets to change the station back. She always wants to communicate about everything all the time. And she likes her glass of vino at night. But she's always there in a pinch, no questions asked."

P.S.—She's not the liar. I am. I'm the only big fat liar in this outfit.

I tell Mom to help me make a stretcher out of the raincoat she's wearing. It's the only way to lift Reggie up into the car, I say. She hesitates—it's her good coat—but she takes it off. I lift Reggie's head off my lap. I stand up. I ask Mom to lay her coat down beside him. I warn her about his hind hip, how it gave out on him. I say we'll need to drag him by the forepaws onto the coat.

She reaches out her hand, then pulls it away. "I'm afraid," she says.

"So's Reggie," I say. "But somebody's got to make the first move. Start by telling him it was all a big misunderstanding. Because it really was. Reggie doesn't know about high-fives. He thought you were going to hit me. He jumped on you to protect me. He's always protecting me. He's, like, the best sidekick a kid could ever have."

I am SO not going to cry right now.

Mom looks at me. She looks down at Reggie. Slowly, she stretches her hand out again. "It's OK, boy," she says.

"It was just a big misunderstanding, that's all." She touches his forehead between the ears. He flinches. So does she, but she doesn't jerk her hand back. She makes herself pet him—gently, gently—between the ears. His eyes roll open. He whines. He tries to lick her hand, tries to make up with her.

"I'm sorry," she says. "I'm so sorry." Her voice is all clogged with snot and tears. Tears are streaming down her face.

I lay a hand on her shoulder. "Not now, OK?" I say. "We've got to hold it together—until we get this done—OK?" Mom nods. "Just keep petting him," I say, "while I drag him onto the coat." She nods. She tells him he's a good boy. She says this whole thing was nothing but a big misunderstanding. She promises she's going to get him the help he needs. She promises, as soon as we all get home, we'll have a big talk to clear the air.

Oh great.

I grab Reggie's forepaws and tug. He doesn't budge. Eighty pounds never felt more like eight hundred. I pull harder and he yelps, tries to scramble up. But he's too weak. He just lies there, panting on the grass.

"You're going to have to pull while I push," I say to Mom.

She nods and takes my place at his forepaws. I circle around to his hindquarters. But before I grab him by his good hip—the one he's lying on—I lean over and whisper into his ear, so that only he can hear me: "This is going to hurt. Probably a lot. But I can't think of any other way. Please don't die on me, OK? I really need you to pull through this. I'll make it up to you somehow, I promise."

I tell Mom on the count of three. At three, we give it everything we've got. Reggie lets rip with this scary sort of scream, but we get him halfway onto the coat. Another big push gets him there. We drag him by the coat sleeves over to the car. I ask Mom to open both rear doors. Climb in, I say, and get ready to pull him up by the coat sleeves. I'll hoist his behind up with the bottom hem.

There's no way. He's too heavy and we're too pooped.

"Maybe I can find someone to help us," Mom says.

I look around. The street is completely deserted. She knows as well as I do that they roll up the sidewalks around here.

"I could call your father, maybe," she says. "He lives nearby."

I shake my head. "Go get Marky's dad," I say. "He'll know exactly what to do. Plus he's right next door."

She nods and heads for Marky's house.

I hunker down next to Reggie on the grass. Together we wait it out.

AN HOUR LATER. THE VET'S ON FAIRFIELD STREET.

I read every back issue of *Highlights* in the waiting room of the animal hospital where we took Reggie for his stomach pump. Mom stares at the same page of her fashion magazine. Finally the vet comes out of the back and takes the seat next to us.

"I've sedated Reggie and put him on a saline drip. He's in a great deal of pain due to a dangerously inflamed hip joint. He's also very dehydrated."

"Will he be OK?" Mom says. We've agreed she should do all the talking.

The vet shakes his head. "Reggie's X-rays confirm he suffers from canine hip dysplasia," he says. "Which basically means his hip bone doesn't fit snugly in its socket. Unfortunately, it's a common genetic disorder among German shepherds. The cartilage lining his right hip socket is badly deteriorated. It probably hasn't helped matters that he's still ten pounds overweight. But the severity of his present condition must have been caused by some sort of physical trauma or accident."

"He had a fall last night," Mom says.

"Why on earth didn't you bring him in?" the vet says, his voice rising in anger. "Reggie should never have been walking on that leg. How could you ignore the fact that he was in such obvious pain?"

Mom puts her head in her hands.

I scramble to my feet. The *Highlights* in my lap falls to the floor with a giant thwack. "Don't you dare yell at her!" I say. "It's not her fault. It's mine. All of it. She had no clue what was going on. Blame me, not her."

"OK then," the vet says, turning to me. "You should be ashamed of yourself. Reggie's options are now very limited. The most obvious being to put him down."

I sit. I pick up the magazine and set it with the rest of them on the table. I neaten the stack. How do I explain? How do I say that I will never be able to forgive myself for this? I turn to Mom for help.

"What are the other options?" Mom says.

"A total hip replacement," the vet says. "Without it, he'll never walk again."

"So we'll do the hip replacement," Mom says.

"It's a very expensive procedure," the vet says. "I can't even do it here. We'll have to transfer Reggie over to the university animal hospital."

"How expensive?"

The vet tells her. We both gasp like we're in a bad TV soap opera.

But then Mom pulls herself together. She sits up straight. She says, "Do it."

The vet stands. He says he'll get the paperwork started. They won't be able to move Reggie for a day or so, he says, not until the swelling goes down. And after the operation, Reggie will need two months of physical therapy. That won't be cheap either. Mom nods. He heads back to the examining room.

Neither of us moves.

"I guess we should go home now," Mom says.

I reach over. I take her hand in mine. I squeeze it really tight.

She squeezes it back.

We both sit there, not moving, crying like idiots, not making a sound.

PART FOUR

EVERY DOG HAS HIS DAY

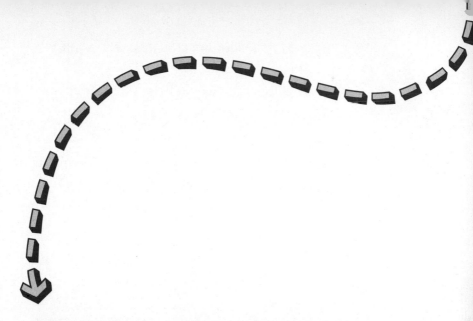

WEDNESDAY, LUNCH RECESS BELL. CHUCKTOWN MIDDLE SCHOOL.

Mr. Gilmore asks me to stay behind a minute. Everyone packs up and leaves. Tim punches my arm as he's passing by. Johnny Hedges and Chris McDuff punch me in the same spot. McDuff whispers, "We'll be waiting for *you* right outside." I rub my arm and wait in my seat for Gilmore to get to the point.

"Come on over," he says.

I go up to his desk. He hands me back my independent study. My mouth goes all dry. I started writing the paper as soon as I got back to school. It took almost the whole week. It turned out to be a lot longer than I expected. I just couldn't say all I needed to say in ten pages. I hope he didn't mark me off for that.

"Wanted to get this back to you before this afternoon," he says. "How does it feel to be back in English class?"

"OK," I say.

I don't go to the library for English period anymore. They're starting a new unit on a book I haven't read before, one about a bunch of kids marooned on a desert island. Gilmore asked me if I wanted to read it or do another paper. I said I'd like to read it. We're all complaining about it—it's sort of hard—but I secretly like it.

"Anything else?" I say.

"Aren't you going to see how you did on your paper?" he says.

I look on the last page, where he always puts the grade. There's a big A+ in green pen. It says: *Nice going, Nicky. Excellent work. I'm really proud of you.*

"Thanks," I say. And I mean it.

"You earned it," he says.

LUNCH RECESS. THE PLAYGROUND.

Tim and Hedges and McDuff are waiting for me right outside. But they're not going to beat me up. We're just going to play some kickball. As soon as Tim got back to school last Monday, he told them all about how I ran away and stuff. They've been calling me Nicky instead of Brownie ever since. And now they've totally decided I'm OK to hang out with.

We choose up sides and begin to play. Townie team is up. I kick first, since I'm the new man and not very good at cleanup. I get a single, which is better than popping out. While I'm waiting for McDuff to kick, I notice Rita over on the swings, eating her sandwich and staring at us.

"Time out!" I cry.

I jog over to her, even though everyone's yelling at me to get back on base.

"You never call anymore," Rita says.

"Where have you been?" I say. "I haven't seen you all week."

"Looking after Julio. The *niño* had his operation. Mom's at the hospital a lot with him, when she's not working her shifts."

"He doing OK?" I say.

She nods. "How about you?" she says.

"OK, I guess."

"How's Reggie?" she says.

"OK."

"I see you've made some new friends," she says.

"You want to play?" I say.

"No girls allowed," she says. "Townie rules."

"Screw that," I say. I put out my hand. She takes it, and I pull her up out of the swing. Together we stride over to Tim, who's on deck to kick after McDuff.

"Rita's on our team," I tell him, "since we're still a man short."

"No way," he says.

"OK then," I say. "I quit."

"You can't quit, you're on base," he says.

"Watch me," I say. I turn to Rita then. "Is that Frisbee still in your locker? We'll just play some Ultimate instead."

Rita grins. "I'd rather play kickball," she says. She runs over, grabs the ball from the pitcher's hands, and starts dribbling it on her knees and ankles like a soccer pro.

"She can totally be on our team," the pitcher calls over.

"No way, Ladybug's on *our* team," Tim says. "We're a man short."

Rita hands the ball back to the pitcher and jogs over.

I head back to first base.

WEDNESDAY AFTERNOON. THE SHRINK'S OFFICE.

I finish telling Dr. Holkke all about my A+ and how I stuck up for Rita at recess. I tell him I've got a weekend with Dad coming up that he promises not to cancel no matter what. Dr. Holkke says it looks like I'm finally settling in to my new life. "Yeah," I say, "but it sure took a while." He looks at his watch and says we're done. I remind him that we still have plenty more time. Mom couldn't make her half of today's appointment because the Ambulance Chasers had a big case to file and needed her to type up a bunch of stuff. He says no, he hasn't forgotten. What he meant was: We're actually finished with therapy. As far as he's concerned, I don't have to come back next Wednesday— unless I want to.

"No problem," I say. Cool.

He asks me if I have anything else I'd like to tell him before we say good-bye.

I consider for a split second telling him that if you say his name backward it sounds like the most famous wrestler of all time. But I don't. I just say thank you.

He shakes my hand. He says he'll get his receptionist to call me a cab to take me back to Charlestown, like he arranged with Mom over the phone.

And that's it. I'm free.

LATER, WEDNESDAY AFTERNOON. WARREN STREET.

Well, not totally free. I'm grounded. Like forever. I'm so grounded Mom won't even let me walk to school by myself in the morning. She insists on driving me there so that she knows for certain I make it to homeroom on time. She can't pick me up after school because she doesn't get out of the Ambulance Chasers till five o'clock. But she calls a half hour after the final bell at my school, wherever I am. Tuesdays and Thursdays, that's back at the apartment. But

Mondays, Wednesdays, and Fridays, that's at Strazzulo's, where she also picks me up at five thirty on the dot. She says she needs to learn how to trust me again.

Mrs. Strazzulo's making me work off all that meat I put on Old Alf's account. I sweep up at closing time three afternoons a week and do deliveries for her on Saturday mornings. In fact, I'm on my way over there now—zipping down Warren in a cab.

At the corner of Monument Ave, though, I tell the driver to pull over. I ask him how much I owe him. I pay him and get out. Mrs. S. knows I'll be a little late to the shop today, on account of therapy. I check my watch and head up Monument.

Sure enough, they're all at the square playing bocce on the grass: Sal and Floyd and Mickey—and Old Alf.

I take a deep breath. I march over and collect up a bunch of balls. I bring them to the old guys.

"Well, I'll be," Sal says.

"I never expected to see *your* face around here again," Floyd says.

"Who is it?" Old Alf says. "Who's there?"

"Your grandson from California," Sal says.

They all laugh.

"Quick, give him a treat," Mickey says.

"That dog isn't with you, is he?" Old Alf says.

"That's the thing," I say. And I launch into my sad tale.

◘◘◘

LATER, WEDNESDAY AFTERNOON. STRAZZULO'S

I'm just cranking up the awning when I hear a *sh* sound behind me. It's Mom in her jogging outfit. Getting more exercise is one of her Columbus Day Resolutions. She decided, once I got back from running away, that we couldn't wait till New Year's to make them. So we moved the whole thing up to October. These were Mom's resolutions: that she needed to exercise more, that she needed to eat better, that she needed to spend more quality time with me—oh great—but best of all, that she needed to check in with the vino situation.

I tell Mom I'll be right out, as soon as I hang up my apron. I ask Mrs. S. if there's anything else before I sign off for the day. She hands me the usual oily package of bones and tells me to get out of there—she's got rabbits to skin— she'll see me on Friday.

I remind Mom we need to stop by the health food store. They have this organic dog food in bulk that the vet recommended—veal and sweet potato. She says fine, we're almost out of granola too. Plus she's been craving a chai latte from the café next door. Now that she knows about Hanover Street, we hardly ever go to the Supa-Sava. Or Taco Mucho either, unfortunately. Oh well. You can't have everything.

In the health food store, Mom heads straight for bulk foods. I go over to produce to see if they have any decent apples left. She's teaching me how to cook. I can make cobbler now. Don't worry, it's wicked easy.

Jenny is over by the oranges.

I've been dreading the day she would walk into Strazzulo's to buy a rump roast or some sirloin tips and find me there. Then again, I dreaded facing Alf Santorello and the old guys up at the monument—until today—when I finally just did it. I still don't know much about what happened between Old Alf and Reggie. Alf Santorello doesn't blab his family business to strangers. But it didn't go so bad, all in all. Maybe this won't either.

I tap Jenny on the shoulder.

"Nicky!" she says. "I haven't seen you in ages."

"I've been busy doing a report for school," I say. Which is true, technically speaking.

"I was worried that you had already gone home to California. I was kind of sad you didn't come and say good-bye."

"I'm still here," I say. "I live here now. With my mom. Like, permanently."

"Really? That's great! How's your granddad doing?" she says.

Uh-oh. Here we go.

"Mr. Santorello isn't my granddad," I say.

"Oh," she said. "I thought you told me—"

"I lied," I say. "I made that up. We got Reggie at the pound. I don't even know Alf Santorello—not really. I don't know why he gave Reggie up. I don't know why he sold his house. All I know is he moved into that home for vets in Charlestown so he could play bocce with his old army buddies up at the monument every afternoon."

My one and only Columbus Day Resolution: When you lie, you always get caught. I've made a promise to myself to quit—cold turkey—just like Mom with her vino. It's not as easy as it sounds. I was getting pretty good at it. I may have to keep a new mental log—on myself.

"Oh," Jenny says.

"Sorry," I say. "It started out as a misunderstanding. Then things got kind of out of hand. It's a long story."

"Oh," Jenny says again. "I'm glad you told me."

"Yeah, me too."

And I am. I really like Jenny.

"Well, the good news, I guess, is that I'll still be seeing you around the neighborhood," she says.

"Jenny?"

"What, sugar?"

"The part about my mom being a really good gardener was true," I say. "She really did have roses and stuff back at our old house."

"Oh good," she says. "I was hoping to swap pruning tips with her."

"Hey, would you like to meet her now? She's right over there somewhere."

"Sure," Jenny says. "I'd love to."

I take her over to bulk foods. I introduce her to Mom.

Jenny tells Mom she's a friend of mine from the neighborhood. I'll be her gardening assistant, she says, as soon as it's spring—it's all arranged. She winks at me.

She and Mom start to chat.

I decide to step outside to see if the little old ladies are out playing dominoes at the café next door.

SUPPERTIME. EDEN STREET.

Reggie thumps his tail when he sees me. He's lying on a pile of comforters by the front door. He's still in a massive cast from his operation, so it's really hard for him to get around. But he's recovering nicely. In fact they say he's the top dog in his physical therapy class. I hunker down next to him to give him a good scratch behind the ears, while Mom heads to the kitchen to start dinner. Thai beef salad tonight. I can take it or leave it, personally. But it's one of Mom's favorites.

I wish I could say Reggie was going to be as good as new. But that would be a lie. Even though he's got a new mechanical hip, he'll always walk with a limp. At least it won't cause him any pain. Anyway, his days of making moonlight flights through the air are over.

I whisper into his ear: "I really miss you at my side. The old rounds aren't the same without you. But one of these days, an afternoon walk will be good for your new mechanical hip—as long as we take it slow. And one of these days, Mom will trust me enough to unground me. Then you and I will go for some serious walks, boy. Just you and me. We've done the Freedom Trail now, but there's still plenty of Boston to explore. There's no telling what new adventure we'll have or where we'll end up. Just you wait and see."

Reggie leans over and sticks his tongue in my ear.

◘◘◘

CASE CLOSED

P.S.—

The three words beginning with *S* and a vowel that make the *sh* sound are . . .

Sure.

Sugar.

Sumac.

▢ ▢ ▢

AUTHOR'S NOTE

AS YOU'VE PROBABLY GUESSED, NICKY HAS DEFINITELY given you his own spin on Boston's history, monuments, sights, and attractions. (Personally, my duck boat drivers have always been terrific. . . .) Nicky would also want me to point out—in the interest of telling the total truth—that puppy-raising and guide-dog training procedures can vary quite a bit from organization to organization, and that every blind person's experience of the world is, of course, as unique as your own. If you're interested in doing your own independent study on this topic, Web sites for the National Federation of the Blind (www.nfb.org) and Guide Dogs of America (www.guidedogsofamerica.org) are two good places to start.

Finally, Nicky and I would like to extend our thanks to those who helped turn this idea for a novel into an actual book you can pick up and read: The Corporation of Yaddo, Djerassi Resident Artists Program, Al Zuckerman at Writers House, and Howard Reeves at Amulet Books.

ABOUT THE AUTHOR

ART CORRIVEAU'S ADULT NOVEL, *HOUSEWRIGHTS*, was published by Penguin in 2002. Hailed as "one of the better debut novels of [the] year" (*Library Journal*), *Housewrights* introduced Corriveau as "a smooth, evocative writer who creates engaging characters" (*Publishers Weekly*). His short fiction for adults has been anthologized in literary journals in the United States, the United Kingdom, and Canada, and was collected as *Blood Pudding* by Esplanade Books in 2008. As a travel writer, Corriveau has lived in and written about Great Britain, France, the Netherlands, Sweden, Thailand, and Hong Kong. He graduated from Boston University and holds an MFA in writing from the University of Michigan. Corriveau lived in Boston for many years and now resides in Santa Fe, New Mexico. He has a dog that looks very much like Reggie. Visit his Web site at www.artcorriveau.com.

This book was designed by Maria T. Middleton and art directed by Chad W. Beckerman. The text is set in 11-point FF Scala, a humanist typeface developed by the Dutch typographer Martin Majoor between 1990 and 1998 for the Vrendenburg Music Center in Utrecht, the Netherlands. The display font is Prater Block One.